John Davidson

The Great Men and a practical novelist

John Davidson

The Great Men and a practical novelist

ISBN/EAN: 9783337031893

Printed in Europe, USA, Canada, Australia, Japan

Cover: Foto ©Andreas Hilbeck / pixelio.de

More available books at **www.hansebooks.com**

THE GREAT MEN

AND

A PRACTICAL NOVELIST

PRINTED BY

SPOTTISWOODE AND CO., NEW-STREET SQUARE

LONDON

THE VERY TIMID GREAT MAN SPEAKS

THE GREAT MEN

AND

A PRACTICAL NOVELIST

BY

JOHN DAVIDSON

AUTHOR OF 'PERFERVID' 'SCARAMOUCH IN NAXOS' ETC.

WITH FOUR ILLUSTRATIONS BY E. J. ELLIS

London

WARD & DOWNEY

YORK STREET, COVENT GARDEN

1891

NOTE

This book is not a sequel to 'Perfervid.'   Although in its pages Ninian Jamieson, Cosmo Mortimer, and The Great Men reappear, they are altogether subordinate to what they have to tell.

J. D.

CONTENTS

THE GREAT MEN

A PRACTICAL NOVELIST

ILLUSTRATIONS

THE GREAT MEN

B

CHAPTER I

A FESTIVE OCCASION

'Summer in Edinburgh!'

It was Cosmo Mortimer who uttered that exclamation one July evening, as he seated himself in the president's chair in the old-fashioned room where his club, The Great Men, met: an exclamation which he followed up by the very striking remark, 'I should rather think so!'

'Of course!' said the honorary secretary, in a tone that challenged, while it disdained, argument.

'Rather!' said the timid Great Man who was honorary steward.

'Of course—rather—what?' queried Cosmo, jumping up fiercely and taking off his coat; but it was only on account of the heat.

'Summer in Edinburgh, of course," said the secretary less confidently.

The honorary steward was understood to hint that he had spoken rashly, but his remark was not audible.

'Has anybody got anything to say about summer

in Edinburgh ?' asked Cosmo, glaring round on the Great Men.

There was no reply.

'I thought not,' said Cosmo, pacified. 'I thought not. I had something to communicate about summer in Edinburgh, but I dare say it is not worth while.'

'Go on! go on!' cried the five Great Men as one Great Man.

'It was a very simple remark,' said Cosmo. 'It occurred to me, as I was walking along Princes Street on my way here, that Edinburgh is the only place in the world where summer can be properly enjoyed. That is all.'

He looked round with defiance, but the fullest acquiescence beamed in the faces of the Great Men.

'Well,' said Cosmo, discontentedly, 'since you all agree, there's no need why I should argue the point. I tell you what it is, gentlemen,' he continued, with rising choler, 'unless some of you begin to cultivate a habit of judicious contradiction this club will decline away and die. Contradiction, gentlemen, is the first condition of corporate life—of all life in fact. For example, it is the basis of the British Constitution. The British Constitution is a triple contradiction—a triangular duel—sovereign, lords, and commons. Contradiction! Why, it appears everywhere from the highest to the lowest—heaven, hell—husband, wife— day, night. Gentlemen, the universe is simply a contradiction in terms.'

Four of the Great Men looked astounded, but the very timid fifth Great Man remarked in a weak voice that it was rather hot, and took off his coat.

'Sir,' said Cosmo Mortimer, 'what do you mean by imitating me? Can't you invent something of your own?'

'I'll take my vest off, too,' stammered the very timid Great Man, suiting the action to the word.

'Good!' said Cosmo with an approving nod.

Whereupon the honorary secretary took off his collar, the honorary steward buckled up his sleeves, the honorary porter turned up his trousers, and the fourth Great Man, distinguished by nothing except his success in forestalling the remarks of the fifth Great Man, after several moments of intense despair, rose to the occasion and put on his hat.

'Very good, gentlemen; very good indeed,' said Cosmo in a paternal tone. 'Always aim at originality even in the most insignificant matters.'

At that moment a knock at the door, consisting of five gentle taps, evidently produced by the knuckle of a forefinger, startled the five Great Men; but the president, without the least indication of surprise, shouted 'Come in.'

Two silent and mysterious-looking waiters entered, and, having set the table for supper, withdrew.

As soon as they had gone the secretary, pale but determined, rose in his place. He took out of his minute-book, which he had lifted from the table when the waiters began their operations, the printed constitution of the club, and read, with much agitation, Rule 6, which ran as follows:—'As this club is intended exclusively for intellectual edification, nothing shall be consumed during its meetings except whiskey and tobacco—the one to keep the brains of the members at a proper tension, and the other to prevent over-excitement.'

'It is, Mr. President, my painful duty,' said the secretary, still much agitated, ' to draw the attention of the club to the fact that there are upon the table certain signs that betoken an impending infringement of this important rule.'

'Hear!' from the melancholy porter.

'Mr. President,' continued the secretary, encouraged by the approval of his brother official, 'I believe I have the support of every member of the club, including yourself, sir (although it would seem that you are at least acquainted with the origin of these preparations, and appear to be wholly undismayed by them), in demanding—in demanding——'

'An explanation,' suggested the honorary steward.

'Apology,' murmured the porter.

'Explanatory apology,' amended the fourth Great Man in a tentative whisper.

'——in demanding an apologetic explanation,' continued the secretary, combining the three hints with becoming originality. 'As I said at the outset of my remarks, it is a painful duty that I have to perform in calling on our respected head to show cause why a rule which he proposed, and which we passed with acclamation, should be overridden in this surreptitious and roughshod manner; but I have performed it, and I sit down with a clear conscience, feeling certain that I have cleared the conscience of the club, and opened up the way for our president to clarify his.'

Cosmo Mortimer was on his feet at once. None of the Great Men dared to look at him; but they bowed their heads and shrank together, like sensitive plants anticipating a storm.

'Gentlemen, you put me in a difficulty,' began their president; and the very timid Great Man looked up amazed, for the tones were silvery. His amazement passed into bewilderment when he beheld the benignity of Cosmo's expression. When Cosmo went on to say that he *did* owe them an apology, all the other Great Men unfolded their leaves, as it were, and turned their astonished and grateful countenances towards their smiling chief.

'Yes,' continued Cosmo, 'I owe you an apology; but I wished to give you a surprise—a surprise which I am certain will be found to be not only an apology for, but in itself a suspension of, Rule 6. If I have your confidence, gentlemen, I beg that you will allow me to offer my apology and my surprise at one and the same time.'

Never had Cosmo appeared in such an amiable light; not one member of the club could recall any former occasion on which he had deferred to the opinion of others. The five Great Men as one Great Man shouted 'Yes,' and looked towards their secretary, who rose, and in the name of the club thanked its president for his affability, his tenderness for the feelings of others, and, if he might use the expression, for this eruption of greatness in a new place on his part.

Hardly had the secretary resumed his seat for the second time, when one of the mysterious waiters opened the door, and announced in a loud voice 'Mr. Ninian Jamieson.' Whereupon that gentleman entered the room, followed by the other waiter with a little barrel in his arms which he placed tenderly on a side table.

'My surprise,' said Cosmo in an elevated voice, indicating the ex-provost. 'My apology,' he whispered with a pawky smile, pointing to the side table.

Then he introduced Ninian Jamieson to the five Great Men individually, each of whom had a novel greeting for him; the fifth Great Man outstripping all competition in originality by grasping his hand silently, and then turning his back on him.

'Gentlemen,' said Cosmo Mortimer, seating Jamieson on his right, and inviting the others by a wave of his hand to take their accustomed places, 'this is an historical occasion. To-night we entertain the greatest man it has been my fortune to meet; and to-night we broach, and shall probably drink to the dregs, the last barrel of the " Dunmyatt Whiskey." When, a few days ago, Mr. Jamieson announced by letter that but one barrel of the finest whiskey the world has ever known remained, and that he destined it for me, I at once determined on the line of action, the success of which is so far realised. It remains with you, gentlemen, to carry it to a prosperous issue.'

The five Great Men responded by cheering Cosmo and Ninian until the roof rang again, and without more delay the mysterious waiters began to serve the banquet.

It would be impossible for the pen of any gastronome to do justice to that banquet. It was a species of satire on banquets in general, unintended on Cosmo's part—for it was of his ordering and arranging—but simply the outcome of his greatness. It began with Welsh rarebit and champagne—'the best whet in the world,' Cosmo assured his hesitating guests. Then followed rump-steaks with tomatoes, mushrooms, and potatoe-salad. After which came another whet in the shape of four dozen oysters apiece with flagons of stout and bitter. This whet was to prepare the way for a haggis, the ingredients of which had been selected by the giver of the feast. Ninian, in describing the entertainment to his wife, declared that the haggis consisted of as many elements as chemistry has discovered in the earth, and that it was just about as compact and eatable as the great world-pudding itself. With the haggis they drank port. Hotch-potch followed with boiled potatoes: Cosmo insisted on every man eating potatoes with his broth. Various kick-shaws then succeede each other, and with every new dish the waiters grew more mysterious-looking, and the guests more appalled, until when gorgonzola was served with apricots the very timid Great Man turned positively pale with fear. But greater marvels were in store for them. After a third whet in the shape of fig-pudding with ices, the waiters brought in fowls, pork, salmon, whiting, interspersed with jellies, custards, tarts; and as the consternation of the guests and the mysterious aspect of the waiters increased, Cosmo Mortimer's self-satisfaction and complaisance grew astonishing to behold. At length coffee was served, and a sigh of relief burst from the gorged bosoms of the Great Men; but the very timid Great Man noticed, with a sickly feeling, that the countenances of the waiters were not yet delivered of their burdens of mystery, and that there was still a prospective gleam in the self-satisfaction of Cosmo. As a matter of fact the tragic farce was not yet over, although nobody could have divined the terrible solecism with which it was to conclude.

Conversation, which had been confined during the banquet to a good-humoured soliloquy on the part of the host, was becoming general, when the door opened once more, and the waiters appeared again with a large tray between them. On this tray—*horribile dictu!*—was borne a horn spoon, a small cog of milk, and a large cog of steaming porridge for each man. With furtive glances and abashed actions the two waiters set the dishes; and then, their faces emptied at last of all mystery, they took

A REMARKABLE DUEL

up positions behind Cosmo's chair, amid a silence that, like the Egyptian darkness, could be felt.

It was the very timid Great Man who broke the silence. He rose slowly, and shook himself, as if he had been a bag of corn. 'No!' he said lugubriously, 'there's no room.' He then took a large double-bladed knife from his pocket, and, opening both blades, closed his fist tightly on the handle. 'I believe in drinking fair and I believe in eating fair,' he continued in a forlorn voice; 'but a man can only eat and drink his best. It will never be said that I, Alistair McGlumpha, allowed a dish or a bottle that the Great Men ate or drank to pass me living. The first man that puts a spoon to his mouth signs my death-warrant. The knife is sharp, and I know where the jugular is.'

Cosmo dipped his spoon in his milk and looked defiance; the very timid Great Man flourished his knife. Cosmo took some porridge in his spoon, and the very timid Great Man clutched his own chin with his left hand.

'One,' counted the very timid Great Man.

'Two,' said Cosmo fiercely with a nod of his head.

But neither of them said 'three,' for Ninian Jamieson interposed. 'I think,' said the ex-provost, with a twinkle in his eye, 'that this truly remarkable duel should not be allowed to go any further. It is quite evident that Cosmo is able and willing to destroy our friend at the foot of the table with one mouthful of porridge; and it is, of course, equally evident that our friend at the foot of the table is determined not to survive the disgrace which the laws of fair eating and fair drinking and his own state of repletion would inevitably bring upon him were Cosmo to swallow one spoonful of this indubitably well made, and, I have no doubt, most delightful porridge. Honour, therefore, is satisfied; and I have to call upon the Great Men to prevent bloodshed by a deed of self-sacrifice—none other than the leaving this porridge unsupped. I know that it is almost beyond the powers of flesh and blood to permit such a savoury dish, coming, as it does, after a supper unparalleled in the annals of gastronomy, a supper which might be called one prolonged whet preparing the appetite for this spicy delicacy—I say that it is almost more than man can endure to permit this steaming fragrance to pass untasted; but you are not men, you are Great Men, and I call upon you to save the life of one of your number by an abstinence which, while it may derange our health and react disastrously on our souls, will redound for ever to our humanity. In short, Mr. President and Great Men, if a proposal from me is in order, I beg to move that the porridge be held as supped.'

With knife and spoon suspended the duellists at the conclusion of Ninian's speech looked across at each other unflinchingly. Hope had dawned on the faces of the four Great Men, and murmurs of approbation now broke from their lips. Still, neither of the antagonists moved a muscle. Ninian perceived the difficulty.

'When I count three you will both lower your weapons,' he said. 'Thus neither can say that the other yielded. One, two, three.'

The very timid Great Man's double-bladed knife fell on the table, and Cosmo's spoon with its charge of porridge dropped into his cog at the same instant. Everybody breathed freely, and at a sign from Ninian, who had resumed his old supremacy over Cosmo, the waiters removed the untasted porridge and milk. One of them then uncorked the barrel, and the other, having set out bottles and rummers, the waiters took their final departure, to the relief of the Great Men who had regarded them with very mixed feelings.

'Mr. Mortimer,' said Ninian, when everybody had decreased the contents of his rummer, 'there is one thing I should like you to tell me. What was it that first started you on your career of Greatness?'

Ninian, who perceived that Cosmo was very much exasperated and disgusted with the indecisive termination of the duel, wished to restore the little man to his own good opinion of himself. He could not have hit upon a more agreeable method of doing so.

'That is just exactly what I intended to be my contribution to the evening's entertainment,' said Cosmo, brightening. 'Gentlemen, as you know, this is our quarterly story night, and I hope you are all prepared. I forewarned Mr. Jamieson that he would be expected to contribute a narrative of some sort, and I hope *he* is prepared.   *I* am prepared.'

In his usual prompt style Cosmo launched into the story contained in the next chapter.

CHAPTER II

'WHEN I WAS HUGH SMITH'

WHEN I was Hugh Smith—all the world knows now that I changed my name to Cosmo Mortimer for the benefit of my soul and body—when I was Hugh Smith I dragged out a wretched existence for some years as editor of a newspaper in Dunshalt, a little village in the kingdom of Fife. Shortly after I had assumed my irksome duties a remarkable advertisement appeared in my paper *The Dunshalt Chronicle*: it was so remarkable that I still remember every word of it. Here it is :—'Wanted, to reside in Scotland, A GREAT MAN. Applicants *must* be great men and Scotchmen. None else need apply. The advertiser has no doubt that the first need of Scotland at present is a great Scotchman, living and working within its boundaries. He hopes the above advertisement gives expression to the desire of every Scotchman. Indeed, he is of opinion that if the hearts of most nations could be sounded to their depths the patriotic desire for a great countryman would be found at the bottom strong and true. Is it not the cry of the world, "Who will show us any good?" It cannot be over-emphatically impressed upon intending applicants that they must be great men. Creed, learning, morals, age, appearance, position in society, wealth are of no moment ; greatness only is of moment in the poet, man of letters, painter, preacher, silent worker, or whoso may apply. The engagement will be for life. The salary will be very large, as it is expected that every Scotch man and woman will contribute, as God may prosper them, to the support of their great man. Application to be made to William Dunshalt of Dunshalt, Fifeshire.'

I knew Dunshalt a little, but was destined to become much more intimate with him. His sincerity in penning this advertisement, and in all that he did, no one who knew him ever questioned. Before inserting his advertisement I called on him, and offered many objections as to the advisability of publishing it. Only one of them staggered him for a moment.

I said, ' A chief characteristic of greatness is modesty : now, no modest man will answer your advertisement.'

The blank look soon left his face, and he rejoined, ' Modesty is the unconscious recognition of one's place and condition. The conduct of a modest maiden is not that of a modest matron ; yet the downcast eyes of the one, and the serene forthright glance of the other are the height of modesty. It would be immodest on the part of a great man to deny that he is great ; so would it be to trumpet his greatness ; but now, when the country yearns for him and calls him, let him come forth and declare himself, not blatantly, but by great words and great deeds.'

I then pointed out that it might be better to advertise in some more widely circulating organ than the *Dunshalt Chronicle*, but he would not hear of it.

'It is not of the remotest consequence,' he said, 'where the advertisement appears. If, as I judge, the hour has come, then the man will appear, although the advertisement were stuck nowhere but on the top of Ben Nevis.'

I let him alone.

Applications soon began to pour in. These Dunshalt did not open before me, nor did he ever say anything about their contents. A large number of them must, of course, have been begging letters. Artful dodgers of all sorts could not be expected to let such a chance slip; and I have no doubt they reaped a considerable harvest, as his innocence and kindliness would respond to every sad or desperate case with an open hand.

About a fortnight after the appearance of the advertisement, I received an invitation from Dunshalt to dine at his house and meet a Mr. Pourie. I conjectured, and I was not mistaken, that Mr. Pourie was an applicant for the situation of Great Man for Scotland.

During dinner nothing of any importance was said, politics and agriculture being the staple of conversation. Mr. Pourie spoke quietly and reasonably. He was a little taller than Dunshalt, but might have passed for his brother. Dunshalt's head was like a reduced copy of Melanchthon's. Pourie's brow was less prominent than Dunshalt's, and there was a keenness in his eye, contrasting strongly with the languor of the other's. The general resemblance was, however, very extraordinary.

At length when dessert was on the table, Dunshalt broke the ice by saying with great deference, 'There is one subject, Mr. Pourie, of perennial importance, about which I would like to hear what you have to say —the subject of education.'

Mr. Pourie cleared his throat, and his eyes twinkled in a manner almost roguish. I was watching him closely. He saw that, and seemed to be conscious of the revelation in his eyes, for they at once assumed a look as open and earnest as Dunshalt's. He set down his wine-glass, rested his folded arms on the table and said : 'All men are either philistines or poets. Children are all poets. Schools and universities are factories for the conversion of poets into philistines. Business aids in the process. The world is philistine, and begins as soon as a child is born to whip and bully it into philistinism. How is this to be remedied? An endeavour to carry out a sweeping reform would only raise a dust that might choke the reformers. We must sprinkle water and clear a little corner. Of all things forbidden to children forbidden books are the most tempting. They beg them from their comrades, they save their pennies to buy them. To forbid the average child any

book is to insure that it will be read.   Now, here is my
proposal: let a cheap series of "Books for Boys" be
published, including Shakespeare's *Venus and Adonis*,
Marlowe's *Hero and Leander*, Fielding's and Smollett's
novels, Byron's *Don Juan*, Ovid's *Metamorphoses*, and
all other books of less note that at present are locked
away from children like costly dainties.   By this means
the unwholesome effects of education would be anti-
doted, and the children preserved from philistinism.   I
see in your eyes the question, " What about the girls ? "
That demur is prompted by a remnant of philistinism in
yourself.   The girls would read these books all the more
eagerly because of their being called " Books for Boys."
Water might be sprinkled on the dust by a short preface, something to this effect :   " One aim of the pub-
lishers is to prevent immorality.   These books are read
by both sexes of all ages.   If they be read in childhood
they will not need to be read at a more advanced stage
of life, when stronger passions might be led astray by
them." '

'This has some life in it,' said Dunshalt, 'and can
be tried at once.   But as to the acquirement of knowledge, Mr. Pourie ? '

' Knowledge ?   Ah! ' said Mr. Pourie.   ' What is
knowledge ? Acquaintance with the names of things.
An encyclopædic head would contain the names of
everything that man has named, besides the countless
names he has given to invented theologies, philosophies,
sciences, which are for the most part mere names.

What is originality? When it speaks or writes it is the power that calls things by their right names. It is the old truth, which, like all truths, cannot be too often repeated—at the right time. Wisdom and knowledge by no means go hand in hand. I would teach children little more than the alphabet, and by that means we should obtain a greater variety in individuals. Perhaps there is no other originality than the originality of ignorance.'

Dunshalt threw a glance at me as much as to say, 'He'll do.' Then he turned to Mr. Pourie, and said, 'By the by, I think I heard you suggest yesterday some change in the structure of cities.'

Pourie saw that he was being exhibited to me, and appeared uneasy. With an effort he shook off the air of annoyance that Dunshalt's question had produced, drank a glass of wine and went at it again ; and again I saw the roguish twinkle in his eye. His eye alone seemed a little beyond his control.

' A city,' he said, ' is the most amazing monstrosity produced by civilisation : that is just saying that civilisation is itself a monstrosity. Consider the green forests that are shorn for wood, and the shapely hills that are cut up for stone. What is given us instead ? Dead masonry and carpentry. Have you ever walked in the west-end of a city after midnight ? It is like walking in a graveyard paved with tombstones and crowded with mausoleums. It is a temporary grave-yard, with beds for coffins and sleep for death, except in such mausoleums as have been lit up and turned into ball-rooms by restless ghosts that will not be sent to their confines, even by "the cock that is the trumpet to the morn." You think of the city when it will be a ruin; and you see that the great and the rich who have reared these streets of stately mansions have only built their tombs. If the inhabited quarters are grave-yards, what are the business streets after midnight? They are empty tombs. In them in the morning their tenants bury themselves; at night there is a resurrec-tion—from one grave to another, from business to bed —and sometimes the hell called pleasure intervenes. Cover up such a life from the light of day. Build huge arcades over London and Glasgow, and light them with gas; they are eyesores to the sun. Wall them round and encompass them with soldiers. Charge half a guinea for a sight of the stars, one guinea to see the moon, and two to see the sun. Then would people begin to know that the stars were finer than footlights; they would yearn for the moon and the sun. I fear there is no remedy for cities but the fire of doomsday.'

Dunshalt bowed his head profoundly, and was about to speak; but Pourie, anxious to avoid the whip with which he was being put through his paces, anticipated him. Sitting back in his chair, he skipped about from one subject to another to keep his tongue going.

'Solomon's words,' he said, 'are quoted in some publication every day; and in two senses they are true: there is no end to the books that are made, and the making of them serves no end. What is to be done, say, with the novels? Make novel-writing and novel-reading heresy, and relight the fires of Smithfield? Get every novelist to make out a list of all the books he intends to write and pay him double what he may expect for them on condition that he stays his pen? Could not the spiritualists summon Moses with his rod to bid the plague cease? When will the people cease to follow lies? I would have both Houses of Parliament remodeled. Upon the introduction of a bill, as soon as it should be read, I would have the members to retire into anterooms, where, locked up separately, they might have time to consider undisturbedly the measures brought before them. When any member's mind was made up, a revolving panel, one side inscribed " No," the other, " Yes," would speak for him to the teller. As soon as he had voted, each member would be liberated. The length and gravity of the bill would determine the duration of the time for meditation. Upon its expiration each member who had not voted would require to do so. This method would prevent debate, which is itself in any degree the one obstruction to the business of both houses.'

The last words were just out of his mouth when he turned pale and started from his chair, looking, as I afterwards remembered, intently out of the window. He said he felt unwell and would retire for a little. I felt a little awkward, and in order to occupy the time smoothly till Pourie should return, went forward to a case of coins and medals in a dark corner of the room. The last time I had seen this case it had been full; now more than half of its contents was gone. I asked Dunshalt what he had done with his coins; but before he could reply, the sound of wheels on the gravel called us to the window. A gig with two men in it drove up to the door. They both came out, and one of them rang the bell. Without waiting till it should be answered, they entered the house together. Their freedom led the servant to suppose they were expected, and she showed them upstairs. One of them who had rung the bell, and who led the way into the room, asked immediately on entering, 'if Mr. Thomson were in the house?'

'No.'

'A man named Jacobs, then?'

'No.'

'Howitt?'

'No.'

'Very singular.'

'Very,' said Dunshalt. 'Who are you?'

'Come, come; it won't do. You know well enough.'

During this brief conversation, the intruders had stealthily approached Dunshalt, and in a twinkling a pair of handcuffs were clapped upon the good man's wrists.

'In Heaven's name, what do you mean?' he cried.

Both of the detectives, as I now apprehended them to be, sprang to the window without answering. We followed, led as they were by the sound of a machine on the gravel. It was the gig they had come in, and Mr. Pourie was driving. As he passed through the gate he turned a smiling face toward the window, and shook the whip exultantly over his head. The two detectives, having released Dunshalt, briefly apologised to him for mistaking him for Pourie, and called for horses. Dunshalt had none, so they had to try the Dunshalt Arms. They obtained a gig there, but the horses were useless compared with the fast animals in their own machine. Thomson-Jacobs-Howitt-Pourie got off that time. Besides all his more valuable coins, Dunshalt had to mourn the loss of some jewellery and a cash-box.

About a year after Dunshalt died. I asked him on his death-bed what was his true opinion of Mr. Pourie. He shook his head, and said with almost his last breath, 'He was a great man, but his morality was peculiar.' He left me all his money, advising me to attempt greatness myself, instead of making the mistake he had made of searching for it in others. You all know with what success I have followed his advice.

When the Great Men and their guest had cheered Cosmo's story to the echo, the honorary secretary asked if nothing more had ever been heard of Mr. Pourie.

'I'm not quite sure,' said Cosmo. 'There was published some years ago in Glasgow a very curious narrative[1] with the very stupid title of "The North Wall," in which an adventurer, called Maxwell Lee, conducts a very remarkable experiment in men and women, if you will allow the phrase. I had a notion that this Maxwell Lee was identical with Pourie, but it's really impossible to tell. My own impression is that Pourie is the Wandering Jew. But, gentlemen, if we are to discuss every story, we shall never get through to-night. I call upon the secretary to favour us.'

The honorary secretary, after several futile attempts at a prologue, plunged desperately *in medius res*, as the reader will find in the next chapter.

[1] See note, p. 164.

CHAPTER III.

THE SCHOOLBOY'S TRAGEDY.

THE room was large and well ventilated, but a hundred children on a warm day in the middle of June had made it close in half-an-hour. Mr. Haggle, the head-master, doled out with dull recapitulation a lesson in grammar. Now and again he whipped a boy to rouse his own flagging energies, and as a check on the general drowsiness. Returning to his desk after one of these well-timed onslaughts, he noticed a suspicious closing of a book on the part of Jenny Stewart, who was that day the dux of the girls.

'Girl Stewart, stand. Come here.'

Scholars under Mr. Haggle's charge were never addressed by their christian names; and as boys and girls were taught together, in speaking to individuals Mr. Haggle, in his own phrase, 'prefixed to the surname a word denoting gender,' thereby illustrating one of the rules of the grammar which he delighted to cram and to thrash into the brains and through the palms of his unfortunate pupils.

Jenny Stewart promptly obeyed the word of command, and went up to Mr. Haggle's desk.

'Were you looking on, girl Stewart?' asked the master in a dry voice, indicating the mark of interrogation by an exasperating cough.

'No, sir,' answered Jenny, with a resigned look and accent.

'I saw you close your book. Let me see it.'

Jenny handed up her book, and at a sign from Mr. Haggle returned to her seat.

The master then shook out the book, and a soiled half sheet of note paper fell on his desk. He tucked his cane under his left arm; smoothed the paper carefully, and read it with close attention. Forty girls and sixty boys sat before him holding their breath : the hundred children occupied five forms, the girls in front.

Mr. Haggle laid down his cane, rubbed his spectacles, wiped his shaven mouth, stroked the thick, gray whiskers that, with his hair, enclosed his face like a faded plush frame, and read the paper again. A sardonic expression gradually appeared in every feature. His broad chin filled with innumerable dimples; his thick underlip dropped to one side; his upper lip tightened; his nostrils curled; his eyes gleamed; one heavy eyebrow rose and the other fell. Two kinds of men succeed, with different kinds of success, as schoolmasters : those who, besides having sympathy with childhood, possess the dramatist's faculty of thinking with it; and those who have neither sympathy nor insight. Mr. Haggle was of the latter order. It was before the days of school boards; so he had managed to flog his way from the lowest to the highest post in the only government school in Kilurn—not the Perthshire Kilurn, but the Ayrshire one, on the eastern shore of the Firth of Clyde. Mr. Haggle hated children and his punishments were cruel: he hurt their minds as well as their bodies.

'Nothing like this ever happened before,' he said, increasing the natural harshness of his voice. 'I'm going to read it aloud.'

'Shame! shame!' I cried.

'Was that you, boy Cameron?' queried the master, as soon as his anger would allow him to speak.

'Yes.'

'Stand.'

I rose trembling, and as red as fire.

'Are you mad?' cried Mr. Haggle, himself enraged to madness. 'How dare you? Such a sound was never heard before since I became headmaster here; and I will give you a flogging to match your impertinence. Continue standing while I read this.'

I tried to speak, but couldn't articulate a word. Mortified and afraid, I took hold of the back of the form to steady myself.

'Don't lean, sir!' roared the master.

I pulled myself together, and stood with bent head and clenched hands. An occasional shiver passed through me and through the whole class. Mr. Haggle felt the children trembling before him, and rejoiced. This is what he read :—

'My dearest Jenny,—I love you; I've tried to say it, but I can't. I hope you won't laugh. Will you love me and wait for me, and be my wife some day, and will you meet me to-night at seven at Bearhope's Point? Whether you like me or not, you might come for once and walk along the shore.

JAMES CAMERON.

'P.S. In to-day's history, you see, Richard II. married Isabella of France when she was only eight years old, and although, perhaps, we can't get married yet, we might be engaged.

J. C.'

Mr. Haggle read, or rather sang, very loud, pitching his voice up and down after the fashion still common among the older Scotch ministers; and the children, understanding what was expected of them, laughed noisily.

'Silence!' shouted Mr. Haggle, and the laughter ceased. 'Boys and girls, this is a thing that deserves to be laughed at, but it is a serious matter, too. You girl Stewart——'

'I never read it, I never read it,' cried Jenny, bursting into tears.

Mr. Haggle understood that Jenny meant to plead

extenuating circumstances. In the awful voice which he adopted when he spoke a foreign language, he said, '*Petitio principii*—you are begging the question. You received the letter and concealed it; therefore you *meant* to read it. Therefore you will——'

Again he was interrupted, this time by a solitary laugh, hysterical a little, but with a happy ring in it.

'Was it actually you who laughed, Cameron?'

'Yes,' I answered.

I had interpreted Jenny's exclamation differently from the master. For me it meant, 'Had I read the letter, I would have eaten it rather than give it up.' For a moment or two I felt no dread of the master.

Mr. Haggle became livid with rage; it was fully half a minute before he found words.

'You shall smart for this, sir,' he said slowly.

Then he picked up the letter, and began to try to sting my soul.

'And so you are in love, are you, at thirteen—and Miss Stewart, too, I suppose, at twelve? It's very considerate of you—such a fiery lover—to ask her to wait. "The course of true love never did run smooth:" I suppose you've made up your mind for that. Did you bargain for any floggings in the course of your true love? Eh? But why should you wait? Why not get married to-morrow? You, with your distinguished abilities'—I was as a rule at the bottom of the class—'will easily make a way for yourself.'

But my feelings were not hurt, and my courage

still held out; with a smile I looked the master in the face.

'Are you aware,' said Mr. Haggle, 'of the enormity of what you have done? During a class you have allowed your thoughts to wander away to a subject which is forbidden absolutely to a boy of your age; and you have endeavoured to draw the attention of a girl to the same subject, suggesting to her ideas that should be far from her mind for half-a-dozen years yet, corrupting her young imagination and making it as foul as your own.'

I stared at the master with a look of dull amazement; I didn't understand him. Then I laughed quietly.

'Go to the lobby!' shouted Mr. Haggle.

I left the room at once, casting a long glance at Jenny, who looked up for a second through her tears.

Mr. Haggle's room was on the upper floor in the centre of the building. It was entered by two doors, one on either side, opening on lobbies from which the upper rooms in the wings of the school were reached; these lobbies also led to the outside stairs, built against the wall and forming the fork of a Y; their united part, which led to the ground, being the stalk of the letter.

The lobbies—one for boys, the other for girls, as Mr. Haggle often administered chastisement on feminine palms—were the places where punishments of a serious nature were inflicted.

Having posted his miserable favourite at the magisterial desk with a slate, on which to write the names of those who misconducted themselves during his absence, Mr. Haggle entered the boys' lobby; but I was not there. Once or twice such a thing had happened before. It was foolish to run away, as Mr. Haggle pointed out, for he was very swift of foot, and had invariably caught the fugitive and doubled the punishment. The importance of the present occasion increased his agility. He bounded down the stairs, across the pavement, and into the street. Seeing no signs on either hand of the fugitive, Mr. Haggle returned to the playground just in time to see me disappearing over the wall opposite the gate.

I was actually the first boy of the many hundred 'lobbied' by Mr. Haggle to whom this simple ruse had occurred; for when an unfortunate was sentenced to abide the master's wrath in that narrow passage, terror held him fast, or sent him off in disastrous flight. I had been there once or twice before, and had suffered as much from fear as any of the other wretches whose minds and bodies were warped and stunted by Mr. Haggle's discipline; but this time, though I trembled, my presence of mind did not forsake me. Knowing that I was in for a thrashing in Mr. Haggle's best style —which meant until the master's arm was tired—I had determined in a brief meditation to have value for my punishment; and so, surprised into a smile at the idea, I had crossed the stairs and hidden in the girls' lobby.

'Come back, sir,' shouted the master, rushing across the playground.

I had dropped into the street before I heard the summons, but I hesitated for a second; I actually thought of climbing back and surrendering, so powerful was the master's sway over his pupils. The certainty, however, that nothing I could do now would in the least degree modify my punishment, determined me to postpone its infliction as long as possible. So I set off down the road at the top of my speed. I soon heard Mr. Haggle on my track, and the feeling that I was being hunted caused my knees to tremble. I could hardly drag my legs after me; but the moment I turned into the High Street, my limbs recovered their strength, and I span along at a frantic pace.

It was market-day in Kilurn, and the street was thronged. The various groups made way for me, and stared after me with divers degrees of unintelligent wonder; but when Mr. Haggle appeared among them they soon understood what was toward. Such a chase up the High Street had been seen on a market-day before. The news that 'the schulemaister was after a laddie,' sped on in advance of me, and the business of the market was soon at a standstill. Numbers of the farmers, corn-merchants, and tradesmen present had boys of their own at Mr. Haggle's school, and some of the younger ones had themselves been under his ferula. They all knew something of the severity of the school-master's discipline, and, although they would not interfere actively, feeling in their good, stupid hearts that Mr. Haggle only did his duty, somehow or other there was a clear lane for me, and a most tortuous passage for the master. The hum of bargain-making had ceased along the street; windows went up, and old women and young leaned out with muttered imprecations on the schoolmaster, and more loudly expressed encouragement and sympathy for the runaway; and yet not one of these dames would have given me shelter had I sought it of them. They, too, believed that Mr. Haggle was right, and that I was wrong, and would have confessed to weakness in sympathising with me. It is very strange! How old the world is!—and people have not yet learned to trust their hearts.

When I found myself beyond the crowd, I turned down Heron Lane; and when the schoolmaster arrived at the corner I was not to be seen.

Heron Lane, a long winding passage, led from the High Street to the shore. It was closely built on both sides, and the schoolmaster saw at once that his prey must have been received into one or other of the shops or houses at the top of it: he had been very close on my heels, so that he knew I could not have gone far down the lane. He did not take long to decide which was the likeliest hiding-place. Old Peter Stewart's shop was the third building on the left-hand side of the lane; and as Peter was the father of Jenny Stewart, the girl accessory to my crime, Mr. Haggle went across at once, and accosted him as he stood in his doorway.

'Did you see Jamie Cameron pass, Mr. Stewart?' asked Mr. Haggle.

'I did not,' said Stewart, turning away.

Mr. Haggle followed him, feeling—what everybody experienced on entering Stewart's shop for the hundredth as well as for the first time, a sense of impending extinction under a ruin of books. Pillars of books farther straitened the originally narrow doorway. There was barely room for customers to stand at the counter—an article of furniture which had to be taken on trust, as the stock-in-trade had been built against it, and piled on its top, so that it had the appearance of a solid block of books, behind which little more of Stewart was visible than his beaming black eyes. On either side of the counter a loftier heap stood up: that at the door, having the wall to lean against, seemed a comparatively secure structure; whereas the other heap, like the gable of a castle in the air, was for ever tottering and crumbling, and being rebuilt in the most fantastic shapes. On the customer's side of the counter a mass of books about five feet high, six feet deep, and ten feet long, lay, compact as a pile of bricks, dense and hopeless as ignorance, and hiding all the shelves except the two top ones, which groaned with old calf-bound theology. There was more room, though less light, on the bookseller's side of the counter; several tiers of books, and some mildewed engravings, permitted only a ray or two of the willingest sun to struggle through the window here and there. A box containing coal in a corner, and a chair on either side of the fire, left just space enough for those operations of cookery in which Stewart was an adept, and which, after the contemplation of his daughter, formed his chief delight. He was, indeed, a much better cook than bookseller, but thrift supplied the place of skill. The litter in his shop was an accumulation of unsaleable books gathered during many years. A Glasgow acquaintance in the business visited Stewart periodically, and all purchases made between his visits were kept in a box under the counter until they should be inspected by this authority. The great man from the city took a selection with him, accounting for them on his return; the rejected books were then arranged in the shop according to size, and troubled the soul of Stewart no more.

Late in life Peter Stewart had for pity's sake married the widow of an old friend. His wife had lived only two years after the birth of Jenny; and from that time the girl had been brought up almost entirely by her father. The relations between the two grew to be more intimate and sympathetic than is usual even between mother and daughter. In the days of Jenny's infancy Stewart had managed all domestic matters himself, and, having acquired a liking for cookery, refused to yield the ladle to Jenny. There had been a fight over the duster and the broom; but at the age of ten Jenny had succeeded in making them her insignia.

Mr. Haggle, autocrat as he was, felt constrained to subdue his overbearing manner in the presence of Peter

Stewart—a tribute commonly offered by even greater men than schoolmasters to a life of quiet independence.

'And you didn't see Jamie Cameron pass here?' asked Mr. Haggle again.

'I did not,' answered Stewart.

'Did you see him at all?' pursued the school-master.

'I did.'

'Where did he go, then?'

'Find out. I'll answer no more questions.'

'The discipline of the school must be maintained, Mr. Stewart,' said the schoolmaster severely. 'I require your support and that of every law-abiding inhabitant of Kilurn. As a matter of duty you should tell me where Jamie Cameron is hiding.'

'How can you tell that I ken where he's hiding? But it doesn't matter. If I did, I wouldn't tell on him. I wouldn't tell on a fox, and do you think I'd put you on the scent o' Jamie Cameron, and him such friends with Jenny?'

'Oh! you know about that, do you?' said Mr. Haggle, with a sneer. 'Do you know that he has made her a formal offer of marriage?'

'What!' cried Stewart, thrusting one hand in his pocket and sticking a pen he held in the other behind his ear. 'Do you mean to tell me so? Ay, man! In our young days—if I may be allowed to signify that you was ever young, Mr. Haggle—we used to say " Boys will be boys;" but now we'll have to make it " Boys will be men," I'm thinking. Made an offer of his heart and hand? Did he, though! At thirteen! Well, well! And it'll be for that you were wanting to send the bit laddie? Do you not think that's just a wee ill-natured, Mr. Haggle?'

'Ill-natured!' exclaimed Mr. Haggle wrathfully. But I won't argue the point with a man who talks in this cold-blooded manner about such wicked precocity. During a class—the grammar hour, too—this child of Satan—for I cannot call him anything else—managed to convey, under my very nose, a love-letter to your daughter—an altogether unprecedented piece of insubordination. I must find him and flog him at once.'

'Under your very nose? Ha, ha! At thirteen! Do you ken that I was in love when I was seven—with a bonny, wee, fair-haired lassie, Mr. Haggle? And I was friends with two laddies that proposed at the age of six; ay, and married the lassies at the hinder end, too. You should never have been a schoolmaster, Mr. Haggle. I read a bit among my bookies, Mr. Haggle; and the more I read the more I'm convinced that there's far more harm done by strictness, even *with* love, than by laxity, even if it comes from sheer indolence and carelessness. And you can put that in your pipe and smoke it, Mr. Haggle. And, hark ye! If I hear o' you laying your fell claws on Jenny, I'll——did you ever read "Roderick Random," Mr. Haggle?'

'God forbid!' exclaimed the schoolmaster.

'God would be pretty well pleased, I'm thinking, if

you were to learn a lesson o' humanity, even out o'
" Roderick Random," Mr. Haggle. Well, you and me'll
act a scene from " Roderick Random " if you touch a hair
o' Jenny's head. I would scourge ye with your own cane
before all your scholars till ye could neither stand nor
sit ; and take a month for it gladly, and that's a fact.'

Mr. Haggle, without replying, retired from the old
bookseller's shop, and prosecuted his inquiries after the
runagate further down the lane, without success. At
last he gave up the search. On his return, as he passed
Stewart, who again stood in his doorway, he said, ' If I
find that he has been sheltered by you——'! a signi-
ficant double shake of the head finished the sentence.

Some seconds after Mr. Haggle's retreat, Stewart
re-entered his shop, and, climbing up a small ladder
placed against his embankment of books, rested his
elbows on the top of it and addressed his shelves of
theology.

' Suppose, now,' he said, ' Jamie Cameron had come
into my shop, and had slippit round and hid under the
counter in front o' the fire, he would be fair skelped with
the heat, and I would have tell't no lies ; for, if he came
in here, he didn't pass by my door, and that was all I
said. And when he asked me if he knew where I was, all
I said was, " Find out." If Jamie Cameron is under
my counter just now, the best thing he can do is to get
out as quietly as he can while my back's turned, so that
I can say I never saw or heard him leaving my shop ;
for he's a fell deevil, the schoolmaster, and I wouldn't

like the laddie to suffer because I sheltered him. The worst of it is, if he is in my shop I must have seen him enter ; he couldn't possibly have hidden under my counter without my leave. Well, that'll just have to be a case of conscience, Mr. Baxter, for you and me to settle between us,' and he nodded his head at a fat volume of 'The Saint's Everlasting Rest.' 'It's a lie I mean to tell—that is, if he did enter my shop—Eh ! what's that ? It must have been a mouse. Ah ! well, Mr. Baxter, you and me'll discuss that little point later on. Mind, I never saw or heard the laddie leave my shop; and if he never *left* it, and if he's not *in* it, how could he have entered it, even although I may have seen him, or thought I saw him, coming in. That's my line o' argument, Mr. Baxter, and you can take it to avizandum for a while. We'll have a bout o' casuistry in the gloaming.'

While the old man, his eye fixed on Baxter's portly volume, was still addressing the double row of divinity, with scorched cheek and anxious air I slipped out into the street.

And now I want to go back to Jenny Stewart. Having brooded for many years over some things that Jenny said, my visions have become real to me, and I think you will find them as verisimilar as those incidents in which I was an actor.

When Jenny Stewart returned from school in the afternoon the market was over. She was only twelve, but she was tall for her age, and something about her that day drew all eyes to her as she walked home. Young men and boys, old men and women and other girls all looked at her with interest. The town-clerk, the doctor, the most reputable solicitor, the banker, and a wealthy but unranked burgher, obstructing the pavement opposite the post-office, opened a path for her with military promptitude, although they were half-ashamed of it afterwards ; for, said the unranked burgher : ' That's old Stewart's daughter.'

' The Radical ? ' queried the doctor with an inflection which presupposed a negative.

' Ay, but she is though,' replied the unranked burgher as if to a contradiction.

Then the men looked curiously at each other, and drew together again, planting themselves with a rigidity which seemed to bid defiance to courtesy and womankind.

One of the round dozen of loafers who hung about the cross of Kilurn—a weather-bronzed slab of granite with runic carving and inscription—said aloud as Jenny passed, 'There's a gallant lassie for ye, now ! ' He was a poacher and had some imagination, as all the more daring law-breakers have. She did not hear, nor did she catch the lavish glances thrown at her. She seemed to waste her eyes upon the pavement ; but when she did raise them it was plain that, like other stars, although they had been looking down they had not been watching what lay beneath them ; they shone through some night of day-dreams regardless of the

underworld. She cared not now for the raree show of
the street. She did not steal side-glances at shop-
windows to see herself—a use every girl from six years
upwards confesses putting panes to. She had neither
ears nor eyes for the black-eyed girl who twirled a
tambourine to the piano-organ of her swarthy mate.
On other days she would have listened devoutly, childish-
wise, and wholly unprejudiced against the implicit
enjoyment of that which comes from the headless hand.
Even fashionably-dressed ladies could not withdraw
Jenny's eyes from the vision that they watched.

Turning more by habit than from intention into
Heron Lane, she was in her father's shop before she
quite realised her whereabouts.

'Hullo ye!' cried old Stewart cheerily.

She held up her face for his kiss, and then went
with him into the little parlour at the back of the shop,
where tea was ready. She said very little and ate
very little. Her silence was so unusual, her preoccu-
pation so evident, that the old man wondered if my
letter could be the only cause. However, he asked no
questions; and she went upstairs to her own room as
soon as tea was over.

She sat down for a minute or two, and rested her
head on her tabled hands, changing the cheek until
both were red. Then she started up and examined the
furniture in detail, as if she had never seen it before.
The room was filled with a collection of fugitive pieces,
the whole dusky plenishing, old-fashioned, experienced,

secret. An inlaid six-legged walnut sideboard, with sliding-panels and deep end-drawers, with ringed lions' heads in brass for handles, and a pair of laburnum wood chairs with cup-shaped backs, pleased her best. Curious old coloured prints adorned the walls; and, more notably, two small oil-paintings illustrating the departure and the degradation of the prodigal son— now, resplendent in a ruffled shirt, broidered vest, knee breeches, and a tie-wig—now grovelling among the rags of the same, with the swine nuzzling about him, hung above the fireplace. The mantelpiece looked like a gallery in miniature with china shepherds and shepherdesses and blackleaded metal horses. She looked over everything, blew away some specks of dust, and set a sprightly Strephon a little nearer a languishing Chloe. Then she glanced rapidly over the books on the sideboard. She plucked out a volume and dived into its leaves like a bee into a bell. Soon she thrust it back and seized another. That and a third one were repudiated. A fourth seemed better suited to her taste; but it also was soon cast aside. Then she ducked suddenly under the sideboard, and lugged out a bulky, tattered quarto. She slapped it petulantly, to clear it from dust, and, flinging it on the table, sat down resolutely and opened it at the beginning. It was a volume of some far back year's illustrated newspaper, and had been her earliest picture-book. She knew well each picture as its friendly face appeared, but doggedly proposed to go through the book from the highly allegoric frontispiece to the more highly allegoric close, smoothing out all dog's ears and placing properly strayed leaves. But old faces tired her, the homely feelings they inspired aggravated her, and she threw the book to a corner of the room, where it lay in, what she thought for a regretful moment, reproachful dishevelment. Then she opened the door of her concealed bed and threw herself on it face downwards. A minute later a chintz cover, whisked off the top of what looked like a large chest, revealed an old-fashioned piano, at which the demon of unrest whirled her like a tortured soul. And yet she was only twelve.

She touched the keyboard languidly, hovered over it a second, then bounded away to the window. Instantly she was back again, and, striking the jingling keys in a frenzy of desperation, began to sing 'The Blue-bells of Scotland.'

Oh ! where, and, oh ! where, does your Highland laddie dwell ?

The surging music bore her voice along. Her simmering blood flamed up. She sang with all her might,

I'll claim a priest to marry us,
A clerk to say ' Amen ; '
And I'll ne'er part again
From my bonny Highlandman.

She was only twelve, but for a wondering moment the woman was broad awake.

She had little knowledge of music, but her fingers danced over the keys. She felt the pianist's supreme delight of perfect ease and mastery. Her hands were

like a summer breeze shaking a tune at random out of
the tinkling flowers. She was in complete sympathy
with what she played, and was so delighted with herself that, trading on her success, she began to try
a sonata recently given her. With much labour
came little speed. Even the notes would not obey her,
and she was wholly unable to lay the spirit of the piece.
Her blood flagged, her fingers languished. She flung
back her hair, which had come loose, and gulped down
a sob at her ineptitude. Where should she turn for
energy and ease? In a moment her face lit up with
passion, pathos, pity, and she began,

When ye gang awa', Jamie.

Having finished that song, she made no second excur-
sion into unknown regions, but sang out with a happy
peal the first half verse of 'The Bailiff's Daughter.'
Then she ceased singing, and, with her head hanging
above the keys, as if her spirit knelt, she played over
and over the simple melody, gently and more gently
listening to each verse; and the quaint song and the
quaint instrument, with its muffled white notes and its
sharps piercing and piping with age, sent the wine of
life fuming into her young head, and she rose, reeling,
and stood in the middle of the room. She writhed on
her heel and stared about her. Something ought to
happen now, she thought indeed. Watching, hoping,
listening, conjuring, she stood for some minutes; then,
snatching her hat, she rushed out.

Stewart watched his daughter until she had passed

from his sight. Then he went up to her room, and, opening the door just wide enough to admit his head, looked about anxiously. He could discover no clue to Jenny's sudden departure; and, as her room was too sacred for its threshold to be crossed lightly, he closed the door with marked gentleness and returned to the shop.

Wrapped in her dream, Jenny wandered down to the shore. There she found a grass-green cushion spotted with honey-scented sea-pinks, and, gathering her feet under her, she sat down opposite the sunset. Behind her the night thickened, and at her feet the sea embroidered the sand with shells. As she looked across the still, crimson water to the crimson sunset, tears began to fall into her lap, she knew not why.

'Jenny!'

Her name was spoken so quietly that she barely started. It was like a voice in her dream.

'Jenny!'

She turned her head and saw me.

'This is Bearhope's Point, Jenny,' I said, bending towards her; 'but it's a while after seven.'

'So it is Bearhope's Point,' said Jenny; 'but I forgot about that.'

'You didn't come to meet me, then?' I said.

'I don't know; I think I did,' answered Jenny. 'Look,' she continued, pointing to the rim of the sun that was vanishing behind a hill.

'Ay,' said I, 'it's awful bonny.'

I sat down on the green cushion quite close to her; but she gathered her dress about her, and put half a foot between us.

'Can I no' come near?' I asked, kneeling and leaning my hands on the cushion.

She looked at me wonderingly, and with some fear.

'You're near enough, Jamie,' she said.

I went towards her on my knees, but she stopped me with a question: 'How did you get away from Haggle?'

Then I told her of my flight along the High Street, and how her father had sheltered me; how I had gone home at the hour of dismissal as if I had come straight from school; and how I had waited on her for an hour at Bearhope's Point. Jenny, in return, told of her piano-playing, and of her unrest, not knowing what it meant. During this conversation I had gradually diminished the space between us, until I sat quite close to her, with my foot touching hers.

'Jenny, I wish I was you,' said I under my breath, after a pause of a minute.

'Would you like to be a lassie?' cried Jenny, with an amazed smile.

'Ay,' said I, looking away into the west where the sunset still smoked and smouldered as cloud after cloud paled, glowed again, and went slowly out. 'I mind when I first thought I would like to be a lassie. There's a picture in an almanac called "Water-Lilies"; and it's in two, and it's coloured. On one side there's just the white water-lily with its green leaves on the top of the water; on the other there's a little burn with two young ladies in white dresses like night-gowns. One of the ladies is lying on the bank, and the other is just stepping into the water. The one that's lying is smiling; but the other one's looking down, blushing you would think. At first I thought shame to look at her; but one day it came to me that I would just like to *be* her; and after that I could look at her. I looked at her for hours, and I always longed more and more to be her; but I wish I was you now, Jenny.'

I turned my innocent, glowing eyes on hers; and they fell before my gaze.

'Would *you* like to be *me*, Jenny?' I asked breathlessly.

'No,' answered Jenny, panting a little, 'I would just like to be mysel'.'

'Maybe girls don't feel like boys.' said I. 'You can like me without wishing to be me, can you?'

'Yes,' said Jenny. 'Had we no' better go now?'

'Wait a wee,' said I.

'What are you going to do the morn?' asked Jenny anxiously.

'Never mind the morn,' said I.

'But you'll get an awful licking, Jamie,' said Jenny, with difficulty stilling a sob.

'I suppose I will,' said I, paling a little. 'But I wouldn't mind the worst licking Haggle could give me, if you would kiss me, Jenny.'

Jenny twisted her fingers in her lap and looked down; and the sunset had died away, so that it had nothing to do with the deep crimson that suffused her face. I put my trembling arm about her waist, and kissed her cheek, and she turned with wonder and delight in her eyes and pressed her little burning mouth to mine.

'Haggle can do what he likes to me,' said I. 'I'll not open my lips.'

'Poor Jamie,' said Jenny, kissing me again.

'Never mind,' said I; 'it'll be over in two or three minutes. Jenny, what would you like me to be?'

'To be?'

'Yes; to do, I mean. Will I learn a trade or a profession?'

'You must just please yourself.'

'No; but I want to please you. What would you like your husband to be, Jenny?'

Jenny looked down at the points of her boots without speaking; and I looked down at the points of mine expecting her answer.

'I wouldn't like you to be anything,' said Jenny. 'If we could have a little house and a garden—and could we travel? I would like to see the Pyramids.'

'And Pompey's Pillar,' I suggested, with sudden excitement.

'That the sailors climbed up in the Reading-book? Yes, I would like to see that too.'

I had taken her hand, and we sat together in silence for several minutes. The sky was gray now, and the water; and the green of the hills opposite was gradually darkening to ebony. A breeze had sprung up, and soon it grew stormy and sharp and mowed off the tops of the waves; and when some of the salt sea-blossoms were cast in our faces, we rose, and walked quickly up Heron Lane, hand in hand. The wind from the Firth pursued us a little way, and, before we left it behind, it took Jenny's loose hair and blew it all about my neck.

   .   .   .   .   .   .

I was the first boy in the playground next morning. School began at half-past nine, and I was there by nine. With my hands in my pockets, I lounged against a buttress, and greeted with a smile the other boys as they dropped in by twos and threes. Some with nonchalance hailed me—'Hullo, Cameron!' and turned at once to marbles or some other game. Others formed groups to stare at me, and discuss my case. One or two began to jeer, but they were in a very small minority, and soon gave it up. When my own particular friends arrived they took me away to an unfrequented part of the playground, and gave me sage advice as to the endurance of my punishment, with practical illustrations of the best way to hold out my hand, and reminiscences of weak-minded boys who had been enabled to display extraordinary hardihood by meeting the palmies—or 'luifies,' as they call them on the Clyde—half-way, and then withdrawing the hand with the cane on it, 'Just as you would catch a swift ball, you know: as soon as it touches your hands, pull them in.'

'I WOULD LIKE TO SEE THE PYRAMIDS'

The departments of the school were opened separately by their several masters with praise and prayer and the reading of a portion from the Bible. Mr. Haggle that morning sang two double verses of a metrical psalm, read a long passage from one of the gospels, and delighted himself with a brief but eloquent exposition of the text: 'Suffer little children to come unto Me and forbid them not; for of such is the kingdom of heaven.' He then prayed at considerable length, referring to the painful duties which sometimes fell to the lot of a teacher, and begging to be saved from the sinfulness that spared the rod and spoiled the child. The rustle that followed the conclusion of the prayer having subsided, Mr. Haggle called on 'Loy Cameron' to stand.

I stood up promptly, and looked towards Jenny, whose back was to me; but she turned, and gave me a glance from her brown eyes: then I felt quite confident, and even careless. Mr. Haggle noticed the by-play and scored it against me.

'Come here, sir,' said the master.

I walked up to the desk steadily.

'Now, boys and girls,' said Mr. Haggle, 'this is an extreme case, and I mean to make an example of James Cameron. I shall not punish him in the lobby, but here, that you may all see how wicked he has been.'

There were rumours in the school of some terrific floggings administered by Mr. Haggle before the class for unexampled offences, but none of the children

present had ever been spectators of one of these special
punishments. A deep hush fell on the room, and
many children turned pale; still, the bulk of the boys
and some of the girls anticipated a fearful joy from the
sufferings of their class-mate.

Mr. Haggle went to a press in which he kept an
assortment of canes. He took out a thing, hideous,
when its application is considered, about four feet long,
as thick as his own middle finger, and with a crook at
the end. Having returned to his desk and breathed on
his hand to give it a better grip, he seized the plain
end of the cane, swished it once or twice in the air to
test its suppleness, and turned to his victim. I had
only a faint idea of what was in store for me: I was
away on the shore with Jenny; and I thought of the
crimson sunset, and the chill, singing wind that blew
the foam-flakes in our faces.

'Hold out,' said the master, and I extended my
right hand. I wondered for a moment, as my misery
closed in on me, if I would ever see the Pyramids and
Pompey's Pillar now.

White as paper, with clenched teeth, but without a
flicker of a finger, I took the twelve strokes which the
master brought down slowly, with all his force, on my
little quivering hand. After the twelfth Mr. Haggle
paused, and, with a great gulp that swallowed down
countless sobs, I whipped my hand into my pocket and,
bending down, pressed it tightly.

'The other hand,' said the master.

I had thought it was over. With a sick cry, and an appeal for mercy in my face, I looked up at Mr. Haggle.

'Come, be quick,' said the master, coldly.

I braced myself to bear it; the tears stood in my eyes, and my heart was bursting, but I held out my left hand steadily.

It is the case that the pain of a whipping on the hand is felt most keenly shortly after the blows have ceased. Just as Mr. Haggle brought down the first stroke on my left hand, the nerves of the right, that had been deadened by the number and heaviness of the stripes, wakened up and carried their entire message to my brain. Jenny, the crowded room, and the sardonic inflictor of the pain were all forgotten; I cried out and writhed, and tears and sweat streamed down my face. My left hand fell after the third blow, and when I tried to raise it I couldn't keep it open; but that was a matter of indifference to Mr. Haggle: he brought the cane down as before, but on my knuckles. I screamed, and thrust my left hand into my other pocket.

'Hold out,' said the master. But all my courage and resolution were gone; I screamed and sobbed, and stamped with pain and the anticipation of pain, and made no attempt to obey Mr. Haggle's order.

'Hold out,' said the master again; and when I failed to comply he lashed me on the legs till I was almost suffocated with my tears and cries.

'Will you hold out now?' said the master.

Bending back till I nearly overbalanced myself, and pressing my elbow close to my side, my knees trembling and my right hand clutching the air, I managed to extend my left hand half open. Again the cane came down on my knuckles, and again I screamed and danced. The remaining seven strokes were given and taken in the same way: after each I tried to snatch a moment's respite by pocketing my hand, and Mr. Haggle lashed me on the legs till I 'held out.'

At the end of this second dozen Mr. Haggle said, 'Sit down there'—a culprit's seat stood beside the desk. 'That is your punishment for writing a letter to the girl Stewart during the grammar-hour. I will punish you in a little for running away. I'll take the psalm.'

'Please, sir,' said three or four girls at once, 'please, sir, Jenny Stewart's fainted.'

Mr. Haggle looked suspiciously at the white face and closed eyes of my little sweetheart, but there was no sham about it. He himself, much against the grain, carried her down to the head-mistress, who, having restored her to consciousness, sent her home.

'The psalm,' said Mr. Haggle, on returning to his room.

The first lesson always consisted in the repetition of two verses of a psalm or two questions from the Shorter Catechism. The class had learned during the session the whole of the hundred and nineteenth psalm; and had then turned to the beginning of the Psalter; the task for that morning was the conclusion of the second psalm, which runs, in the version used, as follows :—

'Now, therefore, kings, be wise; be taught,
    Ye judges of the earth :
Serve God in fear, and see that ye
    Join trembling with your mirth.

Kiss ye the Son, lest in his ire,
    Ye perish from the way,
If once his wrath begins to burn :
    Bless'd all that on him stay.'

The girls repeated first, and all of them, except five, were letter-perfect. These five received two 'luifies' each. They were then instructed to amend the fault, with the inspiring assurance that, if they weren't perfect by the time Mr. Haggle had heard the boys, the punishment would be doubled.

Ten boys failed and received four 'luifies' each. Then the master returned to the girls. Four of the failures managed to pass on a second trial, but the fifth one stuck in the middle of the second verse. It is a difficult verse to grasp the meaning of, and the unintelligent sing-song, which was the chief characteristic of the elocution of Mr. Haggle's pupils, kept on its course regardless of points, and tended to obscure the sense of the simplest passage. The poor girl who failed a second time was a very dull, unpleasant-looking creature with a hunch back, to whom the lightest intellectual work was torture. Nevertheless, she received four 'luifies,' with a promise of eight if she failed a third time.

Six of the ten boys were not perfect on a second trial. With them also the second verse was the stumbling block.

'Cushee the Son les-tin 'is-ire
Yeperrish from the way. . . .

Rapidly running their words together, they got that length with ease, and there they stuck. If Mr. Haggle had been possessed of brains of even ordinary quality he would have detected in the failure a sign of superior intelligence. The boys perceived a kind of sense up to the point where they stuck; there, however, as the colon at 'burn' was disregarded by them, and its force quite unknown, the utter meaninglessness, to them, of the sounds they tried to recall paralysed their memories. These six boys having each received eight 'luifies,' what Mr. Haggle thought a brilliant idea occurred to him.

'Boy Cameron,' he cried, with a sparkle in his eye and a new tang in his voice, 'say your psalm.'

I had been moaning with pain, and nursing my blistered hands—both of them were blue and blistered; but I now became silent and looked up with affright. Like most of the children in the room, I had learned the second psalm many times in my short life, but only by rote, and as I had not prepared any lessons at all on the previous night I could not recall correctly a single line of that morning's task.

'Come, sir; get up, and say your psalm,' persisted Mr. Haggle, approaching me.

I rose, and began, with a sob after every word, and
a break in my voice—
       'Now, therefore, judges of the earth,'
and stopped.

I felt that the line was a good line, but I was
horribly conscious that it was all wrong.

'Try again,' said the master.

'Please, sir,' said I in despair, 'I know all the words,
but I can't say the lines.'

'What Tom-fool talk is this?' cried Mr. Haggle.
'Hold out.'

I looked round the room, at the ceiling, and at the
master; but there was no mercy anywhere. Mr.
Haggle was quite unmoved by the terrible trouble that
must have darkened my face. I put my hands in my
armpits and pressed them tightly; then I blew hard on
my swollen fingers, and pressed them in my arm-pits
again.

'Come, sir: I can't wait all day," said the master.
'Hold out.'

I half extended my arm; but I couldn't open my
hand—it was a physical impossibility.

'I canna', Maister Haggle, I canna',' I said.

'We'll see about that,' said the master.

He seized my left wrist, and holding it out at the
stretch of his arm, brought his cane down twice on my
blistered, swollen hand. I lost my temper, I kicked
over the master's desk, and, seizing a frameless slate
which lay on the seat beside me, threw it at the head

of my tormentor. I had laughed hysterically when I upset the desk; but I cried with rage a moment afterwards, for my dangerous missile had missed its aim.

'Ay!' said the master; 'so we have our little tantrums, have we?'

He seized me by the collar, and lashed me on the body, till the cane dropped from his hand and I had no strength left to shriek.

'Now, sir,' said Mr. Haggle, forcing me to sit on the culprit's bench, 'how many more thrashings do you want? You learn to keep your temper, or it'll be the worse for you. You have done wrong, and I advise you to make up your mind to take the penalty quietly. Next hour I'll flog you for running away, and it will be wise of you not to require any more accidental thrashings in the course of your punishment. That will do,' he continued to the class; ' I've no more time for the psalm. Those who failed will stay in at four, and learn three double verses of another psalm—they'll be told which when the time comes.'

The class was then dismissed for five minutes, but I was not allowed to go. During the interval Mr. Haggle eyed me like a cat watching a mouse.

When the class returned, they were set to writing, and as soon as all the children were occupied the master resumed his punitive duties.

'Boy Cameron, stand; hold out.'

I struggled to my feet, but sank down almost immediately, my heart was broken; and I was not the first boy whose heart had been broken by Mr. Haggle, under pretence of breaking a rebellious spirit.

The master did not repeat the order to stand; but he growled out his other so often reiterated one : ' Hold out.'

I held out my hand slackly, but it fell on the seat; Mr. Haggle brought his cane down on it as it lay, and I screamed with the pain. He then repeated his order to hold out; but I sat on my hands. The master was about to lash me on the legs, when an important matter which he had forgotten in the excitement of the morning's varied labours recurred to his memory.

' By the by,' he said jocosely, sitting down in his chair opposite me, ' where did you vanish to when you turned the corner of Heron Lane yesterday ? '

' I'll no tell you that,' said I sullenly. ' I'll no tell y'it. You can do what you like.'

' Now, what a fool you are ! ' said Mr. Haggle, striking me with all his strength over both knees. ' Do you actually want another accidental thrashing ? '

' I'll no' tell you,' I screamed.

That which had not been present in my mind since my prolonged punishment began was recalled by Mr. Haggle's question. Even Jenny's fainting had not had any special meaning for me, so dazed was I at the time. Now, however, as I had ceased entirely the attempt to endure in silence, my mind was freer, and the memory of the sunset, and the night breeze, and Jenny's kisses, returned to my broken heart, and gave me a little passing strength. Mr. Haggle rose and lashed me as I sat—on my back, shoulders, legs, arms, and hands. It was amazing that I did not faint.

'Now, sir,' he said, resuming his seat; 'where did you hide?'

'I'll no' tell you,' I shrieked.

Mr. Haggle lashed me on each thigh; and then put his question 'Where did you hide?'

I replied only with cries and groans.

'I'll whip you till you answer me,' said Mr. Haggle.

He put the question more than a dozen times, giving me two lashes after each repetition. The master had now lost his temper. He thrust his face into mine and yelled at me, with fierce eyes, knotted forehead, and hot breath. Suddenly he desisted. This was a morning of brilliant ideas for Mr. Haggle, and the most brilliant of them had just suggested itself.

'Stop writing,' he said. 'Stand. Let us pray.'

He prayed with great fervour that this punishment might be sanctified to James Cameron; that the poor, misguided boy might be led to see the error of his ways, and, in submission to the superior placed over him by Providence, tell what was required of him.

At the conclusion of the prayer the class resumed their writing, and Mr. Haggle seated himself again opposite me.

'Now, James,' he said in as soft a voice as he could adopt, 'I hope your heart has been touched, and that you will answer my question. Where did you hide yesterday?'

I shook my head.

'Very well,' said the master, rising; 'we'll just have to begin again, James. Stand up, sir, and hold out.'

I could do neither for the pain in my legs and hands, which yet was as nothing to the anguish of my mind. I sat with my hands in my pockets, trembling in every limb, and swaying backwards and forwards. On my failure to obey the command Mr. Haggle lashed me on the thighs, the calves of the legs, the knees, on the backs of the hands through my pockets; and I sat with contorted face and the tears streaming down my cheeks and cried at the pitch of my voice, 'Oh, dear me! Oh, dear me!'

'Where did you hide?' said Mr. Haggle, pausing. No answer.

'I hope you understand that I shall whip you till you tell me,' said Mr. Haggle, attacking my legs again.

A few more strokes, and I gave in.

'In Stewart's, the bookseller's,' I yelled.

'A mistake in grammar,' said Mr. Haggle: 'the double possessive is needless. You will bring me written out a hundred times to-morrow, 'In Stewart, the bookseller's.'—Now, I shall give you your punishment for running away. Hold out.'

Every pen in the room stopped, and most of the children turned pale with horror. As for me I rolled off the seat, and lay on the floor kicking and screaming.

'What's the matter?' said Mr. Haggle, surveying his pupils. 'Continue writing.' But the involuntary action of the children had its effect on him. He considered for a minute, biting the end of his cane.

'Well,' he said; 'it is always best, if possible, to temper justice with mercy. I expect you've had enough to serve you for many a day. You can go to your place, Cameron.'

I rose and limped with difficulty to where my writing copy lay; and one boy whispered to another that 'Haggle was na' so bad, after all. He let Jamie off a lickin' he had promised him, mind ye.'

The master heard; and the boy received four 'luifies' for talking during class.

My father and mother had been dead for several years, and I lived with an uncle, who, while he had a sincere sense of duty, was altogether under the control of his wife. Mrs. Cameron, my aunt, had six children of her own, and with every addition to her family her mind and heart seemed to have contracted, instead of expanding. It is surely the case that the more claims there are on a woman's affections the more abounding is her love; but there are exceptions, and Mrs. Cameron was one. She fixed a gulf between her own children and her nephew—not in her heart alone, but openly, in food, in clothes, in education; and thus it was that, instead of accompanying my cousins to the expensive private school they attended, I had been given over, under pretence of being difficult to manage, to the tender mercies of Mr. Haggle. 'Keep him to his work,' said Mrs. Cameron to the master. 'He's an idle, dreamy boy, and requires a tight rein.'

Such a series of thrashings as Mr. Haggle had given me in one forenoon were not of very frequent occurrence thirty years ago, nor were they nearly so common then as they had been in the days of the parish-schoolmasters; but there are still teachers who cherish the tradition of education by means of pain and fear; and in Mr. Haggle's time, although better counsels were beginning to prevail, the propriety of severe corporal punishment for every species of offence, and as the true menstruum of shy capacity, was almost universally recognised. It was not every boy, however, that Mr. Haggle would have flogged as he had flogged me. The master was carefully informed of the domestic circumstances of all his pupils; and it was only when he felt certain that the severity of his discipline would be supported by parents and guardians that he did his duty as drum-major thoroughly.

Knowing quite well that it would be useless to appeal to my uncle or aunt, I tried hard to conceal the condition of my hands; but my cousins had heard of my punishment, and I was put on bread and water for a week.

In the dusk I crawled out, and went down to the shore—not to Bearhope's Point, but to a rocky place where no sea-pinks grew. I was too late for the sunset; the waves and the sky were cold and gray;

but the wind was warmer than it had been the night before, and I took off my bonnet and let it blow through my hair. I sat for an hour trying to think, and trying to be the Jamie Cameron who had made love to Jenny Stewart. I set myself to recall the meeting with my sweetheart at Bearhope's Point; but it wouldn't come back to me—none of it except my promise to endure my punishment in silence. I tried to remember my mother, to think of some happy days I had spent during the previous summer with one of my companions at a farm where everybody had been kind to me; I tried to think of being a man, of marrying Jenny Stewart, of travelling, and of the Pyramids. It was all in vain. Mr. Haggle's harsh voice with its heartless 'Hold out'; the swish of the cane; the ache in my hands, in my legs, in my mind—above all, the moment when I broke down and cried, and that other moment when I told where I had hidden, would not quit my memory.

I had frightful dreams that night, and wakened several times; and there was nobody to comfort me— nobody even to laugh at me, for I slept alone in a little stifling box-room.

Next morning on my road to school, Jenny Stewart made up on me, and, touching me on the shoulder, said, 'Jamie, dear,' and looked round into my face sweetly and mournfully. I returned her glance with a shiver, and then ran away as fast as I could. My heart was broken and my mind was dulled. At thirteen I had lost faith in myself; and so I am a bachelor and the melancholy man you know.

'Good,' said Cosmo, when the secretary had finished. 'Very good.'

It was observed that the president's face was very red, and that his spectacles seemed to be bedewed.

'Good,' he repeated almost angrily. Then he called on the honorary porter to tell his story; 'and don't let it be pathetic this time,' he added.

'My story is a humorous one,' said the melancholy Great Man who was honorary porter; and it's called "The Glasgow Ghosts."'

'Admirable!' exclaimed Cosmo. 'You illustrate a favourite theory of mine, which is none of my invention, however.'

'What theory is that?' asked Ninian.

'The theory that humour is always the product of melancholy.'

The melancholy porter sipped his whiskey, sighed, and began.

CHAPTER IV

THE GLASGOW GHOSTS

PHILIP MARQUIS arrived in Glasgow one autumn night some years ago, having walked a distance of thirty miles without tasting food. He was in evening dress, but wore a soft hat. He had no money. He lounged about the streets till midnight, hunger gnawing his vitals like a rat. About a minute from twelve he sat down with his back against the hotel in the passage between St. Enoch Square and Dunlop Street. He pulled up his knees to his chin, clasped his hands round them, pressed himself tightly together, and groaned. Eighteen hours without food! His six feet, his broad shoulders, his curly beard, mattered nothing; he groaned, and would I believe have sobbed, but twelve o'clock struck. His hunger vanished, his pain ceased. His mind seemed to grow preternaturally clear. A pleasing sensation spread through his body. He saw a radiance approach, and a slight fog which filled the air whistled past as the light came on. The light became a figure, and stopped before him. He knew it was a ghost, yet he felt no fear. He had never, even as a boy, believed in ghosts; but he knew that this was one.

He rose, helping himself up with his hands, for he felt very weak, and made a polite bow. The ghost took a step back, and went through a most graceful and elaborate salute, and then said, with much surprise and in a voice like that with which the ventriloquist represents some one talking in the chimney, 'It is most unaccountable, sir, that you should be able to see me.'

'Oh, I am not blind,' said Philip.

'Nay, if you had been blind, I would not have wondered. Pray, sir, pardon me, but have you been drinking?'

This was a ghost, and might be allowed liberties. So Philip replied civilly that he had not.

'Then, sir—it is very material or I would not ask—are you in delirium tremens?'

'I am not, and never was,' said Philip. 'But what have these questions got to do with my seeing you?'

'This, sir, that in all my experience as a ghost, which extends over a period of more than a hundred years, I have not met a man of your sanguine-bilious complexion who has been able to see one of us, except in his cups, or in the horrors, or in bad health. I perceive that none of these causes give you the second sight; and I protest, sir, that I am hugely interested to know whence you have the gift.'

The ghost took a pinch of snuff out of a large gold snuff-box and meditated for a minute. Philip, whose attention had been directed exclusively to the face of the apparition, now examined it from top to toe. It wore its own hair powdered, and carried its little three-cornered laced hat under its left arm. Its eyes were blue and phosphorescent, but not at all repulsive. Its nose was hooked, but a large good-humoured mouth took from the hawkish expression of that feature. There was a pale pink tinge on its cheeks and on its lips; but the rest of its face, and its neck and hands, were of a waxy, semi-transparent whiteness. It wore a green silk coat with gold-facings, and its knee-breeches were of the same material and hue. Its stockings were of white silk, and fitted exquisitely as tight a leg as ever stepped up the gallows-ladder. The shoes had gold buckles and red heels. It wore no waistcoat, and its ruffled shirt of the finest cambric was open at the neck. Two gold-mounted pistols were stuck in a belt worn sailor-wise; and a long rapier with a gold hilt, but without a scabbard, hung at its side. These arms and articles of dress appeared to have undergone a change like that of their wearer. They were perfectly visible to Philip; but the whole apparition had an aloof impalpable air about it, not by any means ghostly, however, as that word is commonly understood.

At the end of about two minutes, having quickened his wits—I must use the masculine pronoun, although ghosts and bogies are neuter—with snuff, six times administered in a manner so graceful, delicate, and noiseless, as to be not only an apology, but almost a reason for that method of taking tobacco, the ghost with an eloquent bow presented his box to Philip, saying at the same time, ' I am, sir, exceedingly loath to incur your resentment ; but, if you will pledge me your honour not to be offended, I will hazard a guess as to the reason of your being able to see me, which, I think, will pretty nearly hit the mark.'

Philip, whose interest and amusement had overcome every other feeling, replied graciously, ' I imagine such a refined gentleman as you most undoubtedly are, could not, without doing a greater outrage to himself than to me, utter a single word that could be construed as insolent.'

The ghost bowed and simpered a little in a manly way, while Philip helped himself to a pinch of snuff from the box, which was received back by its owner with another engaging bow.

' I protest,' said the ghost, taking a seventh and prodigious pinch, ' I protest, sir, that I do not design it as a reflection upon your character as a gentleman, or your position in the world ; but from certain shrewd signs that I remember to have observed in myself during the first period of my life, and which I now notice in you, I conclude that it is some time since you broke your fast ; indeed, sir, if you will permit me to say it, I fancy you are starving.'

Philip wondered why the ghost should be so delicate in the matter of hunger, and so frank in that of drunkenness ; but, ascribing the difference to the custom

of the age in which the ghost had worn flesh, or to some
rule of spiritual etiquette, he was about to acknowledge
his wretched condition, when a fit of sneezing seized
him. The snuff, of which he had taken a good pinch,
was of peculiar pungency, and, when thoroughly
moistened, stung his nose like a nettle. He sneezed
for two minutes, each paroxysm pealing so loudly that
the very stars seemed to wink. When the fit left
him, he said, ' It is true; I am dying of hunger.
I haven't eaten for eighteen hours.'

' Good heavens!' cried the ghost, in the greatest
consternation.

Without another word he grasped Philip's right
hand, and led him away towards the west end of the
city at a pace of extraordinary rapidity, which caused
him not the least uneasiness, for contact with the ghost
seemed to endow him with some ethereal strength.
After they had gone a mile or two, the ghost slackened
the pace, and addressed Philip abruptly in the following
terms :

' Sir, the power by which you are able to see me
arises from the reduction in your animal strength caused
by your long abstinence from food. Your spirit thereby,
like air relieved from pressure, has risen upright out of
the bent and blinding posture in which it is usually
confined by your coffin.'

' My coffin !'

' Good sir,' said the ghost with courteous haste, ' we
spirits call bodies coffins !   But, sir, allow me, as we

are about to enter the presence of a number of goodly
ghosts—my friends—to allay in a measure the curiosity
which I plainly perceive almost equals your hunger. I
will let you know everything about ourselves that
ghosts are permitted to tell the coffined. And, to begin with, let me inform you that at this present moment,
the number of people in Glasgow having intercourse of
some nature with ghosts of all ages, from five thousand
years to one second, must be between six and seven
thousand. You will be astonished at this; but you
must understand that it is very seldom a true ghost-
seer ever publishes his visions, even to the wife of his
bosom; because, without getting special permission
from a ghost, the flesh-trammelled soul cannot recount
what he sees and hears in our company. Besides, few
know to ask this licence, and it is taken away from
those to whom it is granted on the least deviation from
the truth, or heightening of colour in what they say of us.

'Give me this power!' cried Philip.

'It is yours; but many things that you see and
hear you will be unable to recall. Well, sir, my name
is Hugh Rawhead, and my wife is Lady Dolly Dimity.
You do not know these names, though the latter was
once famous in fashionable circles, and the former noted
on the highway, and canonised in the Newgate Calendar.
My lady and I are living at present in an elegantly
furnished house in Gordon Terrace. Its tenant has been
out of Glasgow since the beginning of June. Dolly and
I came to it in August. We are English ghosts, but

prefer to live in Scotland, because England is so changed since our time that we have no comfort living there. Scotland we didn't know in our former existence, and, though the effects of progress often shock us even here, it is vastly pleasanter than in England. Why, sir, in that woeful country, my father's grave has been built over; and I have a friend, a Yorkshire ghost, who saw his own tombstone built into a dyke—a dry dyke, sir!'

'Atrocious!' said Philip.

'Monstrous, my good sir, monstrous! But,' continued the ghost, increasing the pace at which they proceeded, to use an indefinite term for a motion hardly describable, 'I will not keep you from satisfying your hunger any longer, as I see you are getting fainter. You will not be surprised, then, at my servants and guests, who are all ghosts. I have three couples on a visit to me at present. The gentlemen were all highwaymen like myself. There is Tony Trippet and his wife, Mirabel Dufresnoy, who was a nun at Rouen; Will Wannion and his wife, the Duchess of Danskerville, who, you may remember, eloped with her husband's second gardener; and Robert Blacklock and his wife, Jemima Jenkinson, who was a Methodist preacher. I am sure they will all make you welcome, and here we are.'

A footman of the most aristocratic appearance ushered Philip and his friend into a large diningroom, where the lady and gentlemen ghosts whose names Mr. Rawhead had mentioned, all dressed in costumes of the last century, sat round a supper-table.

'Ha! Mr. Rawhead,' said Lady Dolly Dimity in tones of muffled sweetness, 'how late you are!'

'My dear life,' replied Mr. Rawhead, 'I would have been to the minute had I not required to accommodate my pace to this gentleman's, whose name I have not yet inquired.'

Philip announced himself, and Mr. Rawhead's guests were introduced to him, and shook hands with him cordially. A peculiar lukewarmth in his own hand was the only sensation conveyed by their grasp. Supper was served immediately. The food set before the ghosts was wholly liquid; but Philip was too intent on the solids supplied to himself to observe further the nature of the spiritual repast. When his hunger was sufficiently appeased to allow of his looking about him, the others had all supped, or rather drunk, and sat watching him with a placid expression of pleasure.

'Mr. Marquis,' said Rawhead, 'if you can now give me your attention, I will let you know how I came to be walking about the streets to-night.'

'I shall be most happy,' said Philip, 'to know the cause of my good fortune.'

'All who have been pronounced criminals,' continued the ghost, 'on entering the world of spirits have this duty laid upon them—to roam up and down in search of people about to commit crime for the purpose of dissuading them from their evil purposes. This is done by acting secretly on their consciences, and, in cases where it is possible, by a monitory whisper or apparition. When I met you I was returning from preventing a burglary in Denniston, and several petty larcenies in the Gallowgate. I am glad to have been the means of saving you from starving, and if I can help you in any other way I shall esteem it a privilege. Lafayette, you may go.'

Philip turned and saw a magnificent lacquey leave the room. There could be no mistake. This was none other than 'the sublime hero of two worlds, Grandison-Cromwell-Lafayette.'

'To what base uses!' he exclaimed.

'Ah! you are astonished,' said Rawhead. 'But you must understand that, just as we villains are engaged in preventing evil, so misers occupy themselves in suggesting charity to rich men; philosophers in amusing themselves; epic poets in helping sub-editors; theologians in learning about God; and those who in the flesh were of haughty natures, in serving spirits who were more humble-minded. Lafayette is the best servant we ever had. Is he not, Dolly?'

'He is, indeed, my dear,' replied Lady Dimity. 'We got him as soon as he died, Mr. Marquis; and very glad of him we were, I can tell you, although we were dubious about taking him.'

'How so?' asked Philip.

'Oh well, you know, sir, when the French Revolution began, we were perfectly deluged with serving ghosts, on account of the number of aristocrats sent us. Capital domestics they were and are; but in a little while all kinds of low-mannered French fellows, who, although not well born, had been of the haughtiest natures, plagued us in shoals, until the very name of Frenchman made us shudder.'

'Do you remember Robespierre, my love?' asked Rawhead.

'I'll never forget him till my dying day!' cried Lady Dolly. 'Oh, the stiff, awkward brute!'

'I hear,' said the Duchess of Danskerville, 'that he has been engaged by Louis XVI. as boots.'

. 'This is extraordinary,' cried Philip. 'Can you tell me anything of Marie Antoinette?'

'Certainly, sir,' said Mirabel Dufresnoy. 'She is the most fashionable milliner to the ghosts in Paris, and she is married, I believe, to a Highland laird, who goes out as a waiter.'

'And Louis XVI.?'

'Oh!' said the French lady, 'he and an English puritaness who sailed in the *Mayflower* keep house together.'

'Mr. Marquis,' said Jemima Jenkinson in a solemn voice, 'I, who talked so much formerly, never open my lips now except to the point. When you join us for good, you will find yourself besieged by crowds of serving ghosts. Of all these the most forward will be a little, stout, unencumbered, olive-complexioned spirit, who, it seems, created a great disturbance in his time.

His name is Napoleon Buonaparte. He is engaged and discharged almost every day. All new unsophisticated arrivals to whom he offers himself, generally as butler, snap him up with avidity, thinking themselves highly honoured. But I don't believe he ever remained in a place longer than three hours. He is the most incompetent, absent-minded, stumbling, blundering creature imaginable. And the best of it all is, the wretch is so anxious to please, and looks at one with such a pathetic, dog-like gaze when he fails, that nobody has the heart to rate him; and his employers dismiss him with a most excellent character, giving as a reason for discontinuing his services that they are ashamed to be waited on by such a great spirit.'

Philip thanked Jemima, and promised to profit by her warning.

'Dear me!' exclaimed Lady Dimity, looking at her watch, 'how late it is! I must go and see to my children.'

She went to the nursery, while the other ladies retired to the drawing-room. Then Philip, with a face and accent expressive of the greatest wonder, said to Mr. Rawhead, 'I thought there was no marrying nor giving in marriage there!'

'Ah, but, my dear sir, you see we are not "there" yet,' replied Mr. Rawhead, smiling good-naturedly.

'And Lady Dimity's children! Are they—are they——'

'Are they what, sir?'

' Were they born since she died ? '

' Most assuredly, my good sir.   She is my wife, sir—my affinity.   It is the first thing ghosts do, to seek out their affinities.   Sometimes mistakes occur, as you may conceive, many spirits being alike in character.'

' And what takes place when an error is made ? '

' A duel, as a rule, which results in the death of one or other of the parties.'

' Death ? ' gasped Philip.

' Ay ; did you think ghosts lived for ever ? '

' But you said there were ghosts five thousand years old.'

' Quite true.   The ghosts of most of the antediluvians and many of the patriarchs still survive ; but the average life of a ghost since the beginning of the Christian era is five hundred years.   Adam and Eve are still alive and hearty as ever.   It is expected that they will live till the end of the world.'

' Is Cain alive ? ' asked Philip.

' No ; he and Abel departed in the end of last century.   After having had a great many wives, they both conceived the notion that their true affinity was Charlotte Corday.   They fought a whole week about her, with intervals for refreshment, and they both died of the wounds they gave each other.'

' And what became of Charlotte Corday ? '

' She and Jephthah's daughter, desperate of ever getting husbands, have founded a sort of nunnery for ladies similarly situated.   It is said that Charlotte would like Cromwell, but Judith won't give him up.'

Philip was so overpowered by these revelations that he was silent for a while. During the pause Will Wannion hummed a song, and Tony Trippet drummed time to it on the table; Bobby Blacklock thoughtlessly picked his clean teeth; Rawhead polished his pistols; and all four ghosts snuffed industriously.

At length Philip said, 'Where do ghosts go when they die?'

'Nobody knows,' replied Rawhead.

'Do they ever reappear?' pursued Philip.

'No, no! There is still a talk in some quarters of the spirits of ghosts reappearing, but it is the remnant of a foolish superstition.'

'The purest humbug,' said Trippet.

This is all that was told me of Philip Marquis and the ghosts.

Everybody complimented the honorary porter on his story, and the fourth Great Man wished to start a discussion on ghosts, but Cosmo called him to order, and insisted on his telling the next story.

'My story,' said the fourth Great Man, obedient to the word of command, 'is different from its predecessors in every respect. I don't pretend that it's anything very great—in fact I know it's not; but I think it will be found different also from every story that comes after it to-night. It is called 'Water and Whiskey,' and I tell it in the first person, but it is not about myself. The hero of it was a bank clerk of Greenock, who went on a holiday with a book of Mark Twain's in his pocket. It ought to interest you, Mr. Jamieson, for the scene is in the neighbourhood of Dunmyatt.'

CHAPTER V

WATER AND WHISKEY

ON a Thursday in July, Tom Stewart, his wife, his wife's sister and I, availed ourselves of the privilege granted the public on that day of the week of visiting Airthrie, an estate of Lord Abercrombie's lying between Bridge of Allan and Logie. Having sauntered round the winding lakelet which occupies the vale between the Abbey Craig and the Ochils, we turned into an extensive park, walking all abreast, and arm in arm. We had reached the centre of the park, when Mrs. Stewart, looking behind her, uttered a startled scream. We all wheeled round. About twenty yards from us a huge brown bull stood snorting and tossing his head in evident rage, mixed with dubiety, over something. As I said, we were about the centre of the park. A few bounds and the bull would burst through our little phalanx. There was no time for deliberation. Mrs. Stewart clung to her husband. 'I'll die with you, dear,' she whispered—good little wife. Kate would not leave her sister. The bull bellowed and came no slowly. Mrs. Stewart had her husband's left arm and my right. Kate hung on my left.

The bull did not know which to attack first. That was why he did not rush on us at once. He was coming up to inspect us. Having settled which of us he would pay his regards to, he would then retire and charge in correct form. Resolved that this was the bull's intention, I determined to imitate the negro in 'Sandford and Merton'—grasp the bull's tail, hold on till the others had escaped, and then die a martyr's death. The bull was about two yards from us when I finished arranging this plan. I took my last look at Kate, at Mrs. Stewart, at—— No! Yes! Tom was smiling waggishly. Could the fellow read my thoughts? I felt hurt, but not in trim for expostulation. On a second look I saw that he could hardly be smiling at me; for he was gazing at the bull. Perhaps he had formed a plan too. I suddenly remembered an adventure of Tom's with a bull when he was a student in Edinburgh. One morning on his way to the University, at the foot of Cambridge Street, an enraged bull turned up. It made right at Tom. Quick as thought he ran forward, placed his hands on the bull's arched neck, and leap-frogged clear over its tail, amid the cheers of the spectators. This recollection gave me courage. Tom would be sure to have a plan, perhaps a better one than mine. The bull was within a yard of us ; it never got any further.

Lurching from side to side like a tar ashore, and describing the celebrated figure of a series of ten fingers projecting from the nose like a pair of ' disjaskit and drunken fans, Tom advanced a step, stooping to one side of the bull and then to the other. The bull turned up his eye on the side Tom was performing to as regularly as he hopped round.

I had no sensations for five minutes; then I grew anxious. The question was: Whether will Tom or the bull tire first? Again—When one of them tires, what will the bull do?

When Tom began to charm the bull there had been a smile on his face; but a look of agony soon usurped it. The perspiration rolled from his brow and trickled down his nose, dropping from the agitated little finger of his right hand. He had no strength to twiddle his fingers; they trembled involuntarily. He reeled from side to side as if, not his fingers only, but his whole man had been drunk, as, to be sure it was—with terror. And always the bull turned up its eye.

At the end of ten minutes I began to laugh. So did Mrs. Stewart and Kate; so did the bull; but not Tom.

Then the bull tired first. It ceased to oscillate its head, and thrust Tom gently aside with one of its horns, put forth a hoof, and gazed at me. Had the bull divined my intentions with regard to its tail? Would it require revenge? On the contrary there was an inquiring glance in its eye. The inquiring glance became wistful, imploring. It opened and shut its mouth. A tear rolled down each side of its nose. Groaning heavily it moved off, laid itself down in the shadow of a tree and sobbed. I knew the cause of its grief—its inability to utter articulate sounds. It wanted to ask me if there was any truth in the report that on a Sabbath evening during Divine service whiskey had been put into the water used for drinking by a congregation in Greenock.

Within a fortnight I had been asked this question a hundred times—in Perth, Dunkeld, Dundee, Stirling, in Tullibody, in Dollar, on the top of Dunmyatt, on the Abbey Craig, on railway journeys, in streets, on statute-labour roads, in lanes, in by-ways. Friends asked me; strangers—whom, in the course of a casual conversation, I unfortunately informed that I was a Greenock man—boys, girls, beggars asked me; until the slightest spark of interrogation in the eye of a dog, of a gargoyle on an old abbey or castle, sent me away abruptly, shuddering lest I should hear the hundred-times-reiterated question. The bull may not have known anything about the matter; but I, in my subjective mood, beheld that question in its eye plainly.

The reason why the affair annoyed me was that I, a Greenock man, referred and deferred to as an authority, was furnished with no satisfactory answer. It was also sickening to see so many people in dead earnest over such a trivial matter. Several times I had thought of writing to Greenock for a full explanation, not from any desire to know, but to be able to say yes or no. However, the idea of playing tormentor to another as others did to me restrained me.

On our way home from Airthrie I left the others to get an evening paper at Stirling station. A train had just left the platform when I arrived. A few travellers were lounging about. The porters were mostly idle; only some leisurely shunting was going on.

'Hey! Catch it! There it is—down the line!'

'Eh! What? Where?' a dozen voices shouted in chorus at the walls, at the telegraph-wires, at whatever could not reply.

The soloist sang out again, 'Stop it! Hey! Stop it, will you?'

Was this some poor Greenock man flying from a remorseless questioner?

'It's a Jerusalem pony!'

'No, it's a mule!'

A mule it was, cantering briskly along the Dollar line towards Glasgow, with its owner panting behind. The chase was immediately augmented by nearly every idler in the station. The mule took it easy, allowing us to come up round it, and then jinking away a bit ahead. I got exasperated and soon led the chase. The mule stopped again till we should come up. It snuffed the air as I came forward, whinnied, and approached me. It smelt me, stared me in the face, and then, with a loud neigh of joy, shied off and searched among the lines. I was too much astonished to make any attempt at seizing it.

At length the mule found what it required: two lines crossing each other at right angles. It made a polite bow to me, and then danced the sword dance with great spirit and manifestations of delight. The other pursuers stood beside me looking on. The dance being ended it approached me again, and looked the imploring look I knew too well. The poor brute had scented out that I was a Greenock man; its dance displayed its pleasure at the discovery, and was its mode of thanking Providence for throwing me in its way; and now the expected information was not forthcoming. I shook my head. The mule understood, heaved a great sigh, and set off towards the Forth. I said to its owner, 'Look sharp, my man; your mule has gone to drown itself.' I then went home.

The following Saturday at the top of Baker Street, in Stirling, a sight met me that had I been dumb would have made me whoop. A man, ragged, starved, covered with mud from head to heels, leading a woebegone, muddy mule! I shouted, 'Is that the mule that——'

'That's the mule,' said the man. 'Look at him. You have often read of him in the newspapers. This is the mule whose successive owners, while bargaining with a purchaser, always volunteer to tell one of his only two faults, which is a predilection for liberty and good grass so strong, that when once he gets into a field it is almost impossible to catch him. Then the hopeful purchaser says with a smile, " Prevention 's better than cure; we'll take care he doesn't get into a field," and pays down the money. " And now that he's sold," says the other, " I may as well tell you his other fault. When you do catch him he's of no use in the world." This mule used to be in the market every

day until I bought him; and I'll never sell him. I
feed him on a straw a day; starving is his labour. He
gets a week's holiday every year down at Cambuskenneth
Abbey. I cart him down, and with the help of the
keeper of the orchard, lift him into his holiday pastur-
age, and stand him up against a tree. He smells the
grass and lets down his head to get at it; but he has
grown so stiff and shrivelled with his year's labour that
he can't reach it. He meditates for a while, and then
puts his head into the fork of a tree, and pulls out his
neck a bit. He does this several times until his mouth
reaches the grass, and then he begins to eat. He eats
all day. A cow in the orchard can't feed for gazing at
him, and follows him about anxiously with a fear in
each horn: one horn fears that the mule will burst, the
other that he will eat up the whole orchard. So the
poor cow hotches about on this dilemma. At night the
orchard-keeper and his wife can't sleep for the champing
of the mule. It's jaws go like the jaws of death. It
is too much, and the mule is muzzled, except for three
hours in the forenoon. From ten to one all the people
in Cambuskenneth who can possibly spare the time,
and many who can't, come to see the mule eating. The
scholars in the school, which is near the orchard, hear
the rapturous shout of the villagers when the mule is
unmuzzled, and rush out in spite of the efforts of the
teacher to detain them. On Sunday nobody goes to
church in the forenoon, because to do so would entail
the missing of the mule-show; and nobody goes in the

afternoon on account of the prostration resulting from
the strain on necks and eyes and toes for three hours.
The village is wholly demoralised during the stay of
this wretched animal, and the orchard-keeper has
always to returf his orchard after its visit. When it
ran off on Thursday I was taking it home.'

'But you don't mean to say you've been all this
time catching it?'

'No, I can't say I've been all this time catching it;
but I'd call the man a liar who would say I haven't
been most of the time chasing it, or rather him. I
like to call him "him." You, sir, told me he had gone
to drown himself. Perhaps that was his intention, but
whenever he finds himself among grass, he eats. I got
him tearing away on the Stirling side of the river.
When he saw me he sprang into the water and swam
to the other side, and began to eat. I followed him,
and the minute I stood on land he was in the water
again, making for the side I had left. He soon ate up
all the grass he could come at on that side of the Forth,
and then laid himself down to rest. He fell asleep.
I slipped cautiously into the water, and swam across.
I was wading through the mud on the mule's side, when
the hypocritical brute stretched his legs, yawned, gave
himself a roll, and stepped into the river a few yards
from me. I swam after him. He allowed me to seize
hold of his tail, and actually towed me over. Then he
twisted his tail out of my hand, and set off at a gallop.
I saw it was to be a long chase, and was content to

keep the brute in sight without attempting to come near him. At night we slept on opposite banks of the river. I kept him in sight all Friday, and we slept in the same manner during Friday night. When this morning dawned, I saw the mule was troubled. I soon guessed what was the matter, for I was puzzled too. "Which side of the river am I on?" We both asked ourselves that question. You know how the Forth winds? Well, we had got wandered among its meanders. The mule was exactly opposite me, and I was exactly opposite the mule; but we couldn't be sure that we were not both on the same side. A fishing-boat passed down between us, and I hailed the fisherman. "Am I on the same side of the river as the mule?" I shouted.'

'The fisherman surveyed us, and replied surlily, "Which is the mule and which is you?"

'When the fisherman had gone, I wanted to find out which side of the river I really was on, and so did the mule. If we met, then, of course we must have been on different sides of the river. If we didn't meet, then we had been, and would still somehow be, on the same side. You shouldn't laugh. Just go and try to thread the links of Forth on a two-days' fast. We met, and I got on the mule's back, and here we are.'

'A strange experience,' I remarked. 'But when I was in Greenock——'

'What!' cried the mule owner, 'you're a Greenock

man! Then you'll be able to tell me if there's any truth in the report that whiskey——'

'No, my friend, I can't tell you; but if you will come to the post-office with me, I'll telegraph to a friend in Greenock who knows the beadle of the church.'

The mule, who had been standing with his legs a-kimbo, one ear cocked, the other laid back, his eye-brows elevated, and his eyes disdainfully surveying the causey during the narration of his escapade, stood at attention the moment Greenock was mentioned. He accompanied us joyfully to the post-office.

The three of us waited an hour for the reply to my telegram, which was as follows:—

'Some person who had been having a dram, took a drink of the water, and left the smell of his breath about the tumbler. This is the sole ground of the report.'

No sooner had I read this than the mule dropped dead, the man rushed to the nearest public-house, and I went home, neither a sadder nor a wiser man.

'Well,' said Cosmo, 'it's pretty lively; but I never could see any virtue in mere lying.'

The fourth Great Man, who had told his story with considerable comic power, was very crestfallen; but Ninian put him on better terms with himself by commending the story highly.

'Your story,' said Cosmo, 'reminds me of an incident in the life of Dickens, which has come lately to my

knowledge. There's no similarity, and I can't say why
it is recalled to my memory; still, it's a remarkable
story, and I want to tell it, and as President I call
upon myself to do so.'

And Cosmo did so.

CHAPTER VI

CHARLES DICKENS AND WILLIAM JAMES CONDY

EVEN those of you, gentlemen, who are intimately acquainted with Zola's writings, will, most likely, not remember that passage in the preface to one of his earlier novels in which he expresses his indebtedness to the neglected English writer, Condy. After informing the reader how his discontent at the want of realism and naturalism in modern fiction grew into a burning desire to remedy that defect, Zola says something like this : ' I began, and destroyed unfinished, many attempts at stories in the manner of what I then called my theory of the *art* of novel-writing. I still clung to this one formula—to the idea that novel-writing was an art. I was purblind. The scales had indeed fallen from my eyes, but there was still in my mind a preconceived notion of things. My imagination still clouded realities; I saw men as trees walking. While in this condition I chanced to read a short account of the recently deceased English novelist, Condy. It was an obituary notice. The subject of it had committed suicide because of his having failed to obtain popularity. That was the reason assigned at the time of his death, and nothing has since transpired to invalidate it. Among other extracts from his books there was one explaining his views of novel-writing. " Let us not forget," he said, " that novel means new. It is therefore absurd to call historical romances novels. Novel means new, but not in the sense of the newness, the perennial freshness of passion, whether displayed by Cain or the last murderer, by Leander or Hernani, by Alexander the Great or Napoleon. A novel must be new in that it describes things exactly as they are at the moment of writing— fashions in dress, in furniture and speech, in wealth and poverty, in virtue and vice, the newest diseases—the newest development of art being one. Of course, if old things come in the writer's way he must not omit them; but the new are to be preferred. Yet there is one ancient thing above all others the writer of the true novel will find at the present day to be quite new in literature, namely filth. Doubtless Swift and Rabelais, to go no further back, have written filthily; but there is always a gleam of humour, like a pearl in a lay-stall, that takes away from the full effect of their filthiness. The true novelist must write of foul things as they are, and because they are, and not that he may show his genius by making ordure palatable : the stomach of the reader must be turned. In a word, Do not bear false witness against nature ; copy her. If a thing be black, do not call it white because it may appear so in a certain light. Look straight at, close into, and through the cosmos of nature and the chaos of society, and tell the world what you see." '

Zola goes on to say that he lost no time in getting the works of this bold writer, and that he ascribes the crystallisation of his own style to the perusal of Condy's novels.

Well, that hasn't much to do with my story; but it introduces Condy to you in a fairly interesting way, I hope. Now for my narrative.

Charles Dickens was in the morning of his fame. 'Pickwick,' 'Nickleby,' 'Oliver Twist,' and 'The Old Curiosity Shop' had streamed from those sunbeams, his quills, that seemed to have an exhaustless source of joy and sadness in the glowing sun of his heart, drawing from the earth its tears and from some quaint skyey quarter its laughter. On Saturday, July 4, 1841—I remember the date exactly—eight days after he had been made a burgher of Edinburgh, Dickens drove from Craigcrook with its owner, Lord Jeffrey, to make a public appearance in the Theatre Royal. The carriage arrived at the theatre about nine o'clock. Lord Jeffrey appeared in the box reserved for his guest and himself at nine exactly; Dickens, not for half an hour after. When he joined Jeffrey the latter said, ' You look tired. Have they been submitting you to that modern improvement upon the rack, a series of hand-shakings ? '

' Yes,' replied Dickens, who was pale but quite collected. I have been on the rack.'

And so he had. When the carriage stopped at the

theatre, the expectant crowd surged round it in spite of the efforts of the police to keep a passage clear between it and the box-entrance. Jeffrey's footman managed to open the carriage-door and his master got out; but, before he could turn, as he intended, to give Dickens his hand, he was hustled aside, away from his servant, and into the theatre, supposing that Dickens was following. And, being an old man, unable to battle with a crowd, Jeffrey hurried to his box, where he sat alone during the half-hour of his separation from Dickens, without the least anxiety, believing that the enthusiasm of his admirers detained the young novelist. It was far otherwise. Dickens did not leave the carriage after Jeffrey; for the door was slammed to, and he was driven off at a rapid rate, to the stupefaction of the coachman, who had descended to assist the police and his fellow-servant.

The new driver turned into Rose Street—one of the quietest in the neighbourhood—drew up about the middle of it, lowered the carriage blinds, and placed himself opposite Dickens, who sat up with both hands clenched and resting on his knees.

None of the crowd at the theatre door, Lord Jeffrey's servant included, knew that Dickens had not left the carriage; and when it drove away the people pushed and strained their necks and shouted; and some said afterwards that they had seen him, and some confessed that they hadn't; but all believed that Dickens entered the theatre immediately after Jeffrey.

By the time the two servants had made way through

the crowd the carriage was out of sight. They ran up Leith Walk and into Princes Street. Opposite the Register they divided, one going over the North Bridge, the other along Princes Street, each of them accompanied by a policeman and a crowd of idlers.

The stranger was silent for a quarter of an hour after seating himself opposite Dickens; and then, replying to the interrogation in the eyes of his *vis-à-vis*, said ' My name is Condy. Will you sign this ? '

Dickens took the paper offered him and read aloud, the stranger having half raised one of the blinds.

' I, Charles Dickens, author of the " Posthumous Papers of the Pickwick Club," " The Adventures of Nicholas Nickleby," etc., hereby promise on soul and conscience to publish no more of my writings at present in manuscript, and to write nothing more for publication in my lifetime or posthumously : and, in lieu of possible earnings for literary work, I hereby accept from William James Condy the title-deeds of his estate of Thurston, in Surrey, England, the rent-roll of which is valued at 10,000*l.* per annum ; this revenue at a month's date from the day of the signature of this to be to me and my heirs perpetually.'

' Why should I sign this, Mr. Condy ? '

' Have you read any of my novels ? '

' Yes,' answered Dickens. ' If you are the Mr. Condy who writes novels, I have.'

' You perceived that their style is the negative to your positive.'

'I believe that if two things can be more opposite than the poles, they are our styles.'

Are you aware that before you absorbed all popularity my novels were gradually forcing a way for themselves; but that since your prodigious vogue no one reads them?'

'I was not aware of that; but I will tell you frankly that I am not sorry for it, because I think that your novels are very pestilent productions.'

'I should imagine that to be your opinion. Can you not now understand why I make this offer?'

'I think I can. You are so possessed with a desire for popularity, or you are such a fanatical believer in the truth of your own writings, or you are so much of both, that you are willing to give yourself better opportunities of acquiring the popularity you burn for, and of disseminating your monstrous social and literary ethics, by buying the silence of him you consider your greatest rival at the expense of your worldly all.'

'You put it pretty fairly,' rejoined Condy, 'except that popularity is with me not an end, but the necessary accompaniment of the spread of my ideas. Now, when I first found you injuring my popularity, I thought to make you the same offer as I make now, but the stipulation to be that you should write in my style. I concluded, however, from a closer study of your works that you could never write otherwise than you do; and so I resolved, if possible, to stop your pen altogether. I have followed you since you left London, seeking an opportunity to get you alone, and I have only succeeded now by the merest chance.'

'How is that? You might have written to me, asking an interview, which I would have been delighted to give you.'

'You do not understand. If you refuse to sign this you will.'

'I will not sign it.'

The refusal was hardly uttered when Condy seized Dickens's right wrist in his left hand, and presented a pistol which he held in the other at his head, saying, 'Cry out, and I shoot you. You feel my grasp; it is like a vice. I could squeeze your hand till the blood sprang from under your finger-nails. You are in my power. No one will think of searching for the carriage at such a short distance from the theatre. Should I kill you, I would divest myself of this cloak, this wig, and this false nose, go to the theatre where you expected an ovation to-night, and to-morrow return to London to continue my literary work unopposed. This is what I meant by getting you alone. I can trust you. Sign this and you live.'

'I will not sign it.'

'Then you must die. There is not one character in all your novels and sketches true to nature, and the world is devouring your writings; therefore, as a false prophet, you deserve to die. Your humour is that of an inspired city arab; your pathos, a hybrid produced from the intellect of a man, and the emotion of a prize Sunday school boy. Your tragedy is melodrama, taken down to the abyss, and there horrorised by depth of brutality. Your comedy is farce on stilts as high as steeples. In short, all your people are yourself in their circumstances—you with your little soul, your soft heart, your narrow intellect—and your genius. The last is your fault, and on account of it you must die. We shall have no more Lilliputians made interesting, no more insipid prattle made amusing, no more beasts made awful by your genius. You must die to make room for men.'

'Shall I not have one word in my defence?'

'I know nothing that you could say, but you may try. One word.'

'You say my people are myself. So are Shakespeare's—himself in their circumstances of time, place, education—of age, sex, capacity.'

'That is so. But Shakespeare was a dramatist; you profess to be a novelist. Besides, Shakespeare's genius inspired a man, your genius inspires a pigmy. You must die.'

Dickens had referred to Shakespeare merely to gain time. He was sorry now that his hope of an interesting adventure had led him into such a box, and that he had not obeyed his first impulse to open the window and shout the moment the carriage drove off. But there was never a readier man in an emergency than Dickens. He remembered immediately that while visiting a lunatic asylum he had by a glance been able to quell the most furious of its inmates. He had no doubt that Condy was mad. Summoning by an effort of his powerful will a calm look into his eyes, he fixed them on those of the would-be murderer. It was not a stare. An observer might have thought the expression careless or even dull; but its effect on Condy was not in keeping with indifference. He was bound by it. His grasp relaxed. Dickens held up his forefinger monitorily in his face. That completed his subjection—which was so sudden that his vanquisher himself wondered. Condy's right arm had fallen by his side. Dickens raised it, and gently loosening the fingers, possessed himself of the pistol. Retaining it at full cock, but not presenting it, he said, 'Now, Mr. Condy, you see my time has not come yet. Open the carriage door, and go out.'

Condy hesitated. Dickens did not raise the pistol. He still trusted to his eyes. Intensifying their gaze, and pointing with his left hand, he repeated, 'Open the door, and go out.'

Condy obeyed in silence. When he stood in the street Dickens addressed him from the carriage window.

'Sir,' he said, 'you are a disappointed man, and I forgive you. You have 10,000*l.* a year and write novels for popularity. You are a fool. If you wish for true fame—fame is not the word. If you wish to be a blessing and to be blessed, spend your time and your fortune in ameliorating the condition of the poor. You seek to reform novel-writing by making it naturalistic: a higher labour would be to reform our poorhouses, our hospitals, our philanthropic institutions and societies,

and make them really what they profess to be. They
are in countless instances whited sepulchres; scrape off
the whitewash, sweep out the dead men's bones, and
make them clean and healthy, and so earn the praise
of mankind to the end of time. This is one thing to do.
There are many. Why, sir, a man with 10,000*l.* a year
might, having only half your intellect, half your muscle,
half your blood, make himself virtual king of Britain.
You are worse than insane to despair because your
novels do not succeed. If you must follow literature,
let it be a nobler path—the novel is among the lowest.
Write a great epic. Spend all your life on it. Reform
the acting drama. Slay the meretricious gipsy that
flaunts in the stolen robe of criticism. Act, and you
will not despair. As for this little passage between us,
it shall never be made public by me, nor shall I tell it
to anyone as a secret. Rely on this, and farewell.'

Dickens held out his hand, and Condy took it with
a dazed look.

'Farewell,' Dickens repeated, 'and may God bless
you.'

Condy walked away without replying. When he
was out of sight Dickens mounted the coachman's box
and drove back to the theatre. Jeffrey's servants, who
had returned from their bootless chase, saw their
master's property approaching, and actually trembled
when they recognised the driver.

'I thought. sir,' said the coachman, 'that you were
in the theatre.'

'Ah,' said Dickens, 'this is a little joke of mine. I am a great conjurer. Keep it to yourselves,' giving them half-a-sovereign apiece.

'Look at that fool,' said one bystander to another in a loud whisper. 'He thinks his lang hair'll mak' him anither Dickens. I wadna' won'ner, noo, if he thocht he wad be mista'en for Charlie.'

Dickens overheard and smiled. His critic continued, 'It'll no' dae, my man. Smiles an' lang hair, an' a strut like a bantam-cock'll no' mak' ye a genius.'

Dickens passed on, very much amused. When he appeared in Jeffrey's box the whole audience rose and cheered him, and the orchestra struck up 'Charlie is my Darling.' Almost at the same instant William James Condy, as was to have been expected from the eccentricity and insanity which his name indicates, blew his brains out in the hotel where he had been staying.

'But,' said the fourth Great Man, when Cosmo had finished, 'I never heard of Condy before.'

'You haven't heard of everybody,' said Cosmo tartly. 'You may as well doubt that Sauerteig, Shandy, or the Cid Hamet Benengeli, ever existed, as that William James Condy blew his brains out in a hotel in Princes Street.'

Then he called upon the honorary steward, who told a story of his friend, Harry Court, which will be found in the next chapter. Being a timid man, the honorary steward's story was brief.

CHAPTER VII

A THEORY OF PRACTICAL JOKES

HARRY COURT was probably the most methodical and scientific pursuer of fun that ever existed. He made practical joking a special study. According to him there were three species of practical joke—the involuntary, the intentional, and the premeditated intentional.

'The involuntary practical joke,' he used to say, 'is of common occurrence in these latitudes. Absent-mindedness is, as a rule, the soil from which it springs. All practical jokes ought to be of a pungent, but also of a sweet, perfume. Now, there is one form of the involuntary species which has become so rank and so malodorous as to partake of the nature of a weed. I allude to the leaving in clubs, in banks, after dinners, and on the dismissal of every kind of meeting, a brand-new silk umbrella in place of a fine old cotton one. You see both the umbrella-owners are victims to a joke of that kind. And the good, honest, absent-minded old gentleman who gets the silk umbrella is the most victimised. He who goes off mistakenly with the cotton article, merely ejaculates on discovering the change, gives it to his children to play at keeping house with, buys a new silk one, and thinks no more of the matter. Whereas he who has so unfortunately lost the cherished heirloom of his family, the great, old, household hand-tent, white with the storms of many winters, and puffed out with the corpulence of age, endures days and even weeks of agony. Absent-minded he knows he must have been, and very absent-minded indeed, to be content even for the short time it took him to get home, with a smally, slim-waisted concern, instead of the sturdy companion of his life-journey; but of this he is sure: had his dear, old, buxom, blowsy "mush" been in the stand, he would have seen it, and brought it away in spite of his absent-mindedness. He does not think for an instant but that he has been robbed, yet he cannot show such distrust of his friends as to inquire of them after his revered rain-fetish. The sorrow-stricken man may advertise for the recovery of " an ivory-handled umbrella of antique workmanship," but he knows pretty surely that, whoever has it, after burdening his conscience with theft, will not be likely to make himself miserable for the remainder of his days by sur-rendering such a coveted specimen of the taste of our ancestors. His condition of mind is truly frightful; and if, as often happens, the prim, paltry, paragon affair of silk, which he is forced to put up with in place of his splendid, hoary, old, full-bodied, parish-beadle of a *parapluie*, has the initials or name of its owner en-graved on the stick, then the struggle which takes place between a vengeful desire to expose the thief and recover his property, and his better nature whispering him to shield the fault of his friend, well-nigh drives him crazy. To the lasting credit of humanity, victory, as a rule, declares itself on the side of forbearance. With a heart full of gratitude that he is enabled to do to others as he would be done by, the poor man gives up all hope of ever seeing his beloved pocket-tabernacle again; and, with resolute screw-driver or knife, obliterates the name of the false friend who has robbed him, thereby annihilating for ever the only evidence that could aid in the recovery of his stolen stack of whalebone.'

'I was once a martyr myself,' Harry would continue, 'to a practical joke which partook of the nature of all three kinds. Egberton, Dimstar and I were in the habit of meeting in Egberton's rooms every Friday evening. On one of these occasions, as we were sitting talking about the ladies, I told how I had recently desisted from a rather serious flirtation with a Miss Sharp on account of my having discovered that she was a bit of a vixen. They twitted me considerably, talked about burnt bairns dreading the fire, and got me, as they thought, into a bit of a passion.

'"We'll see who's afraid," I cried. "I'll go out, speak to the first lady I meet, and on some pretext or other bring her here."

'"Go," said Egberton. "You can only harm yourself. If you get a night in a cell for your impudence, serve you right."

'I went and returned in five minutes with a well-dressed, thickly veiled young lady, and electrified them by saying, "Gentlemen, allow me to present to you my future wife. Be seated, darling. You must be astonished when you think of the style in which I talked of the fair sex a few minutes ago. Darling, you are not angry with me for bringing you here?"

'"No, Harry; not in the least. Your friends must be my friends, and your humours must please me."

'The voice was that of a woman, and they were mystified.

'"Stand up," said I. "Walk about, and let them see your figure."

'"Harry, for shame!"

'"No, dear, you've nothing to be ashamed of. Besides, it's my humour."

'"Yes, but I'll not gratify it."

'"Well, well; it doesn't matter. Now, gentlemen, you see I have perpetrated what you suppose to be an intentional practical joke; that is, I told you it occurred to me to speak to the first lady I should meet on going out, and to bring her here, and I appear to have done so. It is really, however, a premeditated practical joke. Charley Sharp, the brother of my old flame, and I are great friends, although I am 'out' with his sister. He and I premeditated this joke. This is Charley in his sister's dress. Take off your veil, Charley."

'The figure unveiled, and I fell to the floor flat on my back, nearly breaking my head against the wall.

Miss Sharp, and not Charley, walked out of the room in silence. It came out that Charley, to improve the joke, had told his sister that I repented of having forsaken her, and had deputed him to request a meeting. Miss Sharp, being in her thirtieth year, and stoutly determined to have a husband, took, unwittingly, her brother's place. I made her the amplest apologies; but her mother would hear of nothing but marriage. I had to wed her; and that is where the involuntary part of the joke came in.'

'That has certainly the merit of being short,' said Cosmo, who admired everything in the shape of theory.

All eyes were now turned to the very timid fifth Great Man, but his were fixed upon the table. Cosmo shrugged his shoulders, as much as to say : 'It's no good asking him.' He waited a full minute, however; but the very timid fifth Great Man made no sign.

'Mr. Jamieson,' said Cosmo, 'we are all expectation.'

'Might I ask Mr. Jamieson if his son has had any more adventures ? ' said the honorary secretary.

'Not to my knowledge,' said Ninian. 'I expect, however, that he will do something extraordinary shortly, for every moment that he can get from his lessons he spends among my novels.'

'You will communicate with us, I hope, if he undertakes any more adventures,' said the secretary.

Ninian replied that he would, and then drew a manuscript from his breast-pocket.

'I hope you will allow me to read this,' he said. 'It is called "Eagle's Shadow," and is a very curious production.'

'By all means,' said Cosmo. 'Reading is forbidden to members of the club, but we extend every privilege to our guests.'

'Thank you,' said Ninian, and began his manuscript.

CHAPTER VIII

EAGLE'S SHADOW

THE progress of Ebenezer Eaglesham in the office of Messrs. Clay, Clod and McLatchy was unromantically slow. It took him thirteen years to climb to a stool of his own before a desk of his own in the immediate neighbourhood of the confidential clerk, with a set of books to keep and a key of the private safe. He had started from a niche behind the stove. There, as office-boy, during numerous short intervals between his multifarious duties, he had rubbed into the wall with the dirt of his jacket and the grease of his hair a permanent impression of his head and shoulder, known in the office as 'Eagle's Shadow.'

At twenty-six, with 'the confidence of his employers,' a hundred a year, and an entire fortnight at midsummer to do what he liked in, he experienced for the first time in his life a feeling of manhood, and was moderately well satisfied. Having never had so long a holiday before, he made great preparations for it. As it rained the whole time it was lucky for him that he took some books with him—some stories of adventure, Froude's 'Oceana,' and Spencer's 'Study of Sociology,' and a book on language—for he was anxious to improve himself. The book that had the greatest effect upon him was Spencer's, of course; and I'll be glad if you'll bear that fact in mind, gentlemen.

On returning to his stool Ebenezer found that he would require for some days to spend an extra hour or two in posting his books. At six o'clock, therefore, on the evening of the day on which he resumed work, he was alone in the office. He had been copying an invoice into a huge fat volume, and it was not until the scratching of his pen had ceased with the completion of the copy that he perceived his solitude. He shook himself, yawned, slid off his stool, and lounged out of the space railed off for the confidential clerk and himself, and looked about him in the common office.

Seven hours of the musty smell of sheepskin binding, mingled with the more pungent odour of red ink, had not overcome a spice of novelty in the routine interrupted for a fortnight, and in the dingy room, the aspect of which had not once crossed his mind during his holiday. He examined with subdued interest a curious mark on the lid of a desk which had once been his. He even traced its course with a lead-pencil, as he had been in the habit of doing in the past. He wrote his initials with his finger in the dust on a table where a jug of water and a foggy-looking tumbler stood. Then he sat down in an armchair beside the stove, and looked across at 'Eagle's Shadow.' It was a very black mark now, for, though still called after him, each succeeding office-boy had given it another coat. There was no fire in the stove; so he leant his arms on the top of it, and gazed silently at the rough silhouette on the wall. His life rose up before him, and he became very sombre. For about an hour he sat staring at the crude shape. Shortly after seven he started, rubbed his eyes, and glared across the stove in the greatest astonishment. Then he rubbed his eyes again, but the source of his astonishment remained.

The shape had become a little boy reading a book.

The boy looked up and said, 'Hillo!'

'Hillo!' echoed Eaglesham mechanically.

'Who are you?' said the boy.

'Ebenezer Eaglesham. Who are you?'

'I'm the son of Mr. Herbert Spencer's "independent observer." Where am I?'

'This is the office of Messrs. Clay, Clod, and McLatchy.'

'What funny names?' said the boy, laughing. 'Do you know my father?'

'I've read about him in Mr. Spencer's "Study of Sociology."'

'Have you, now? What a clever man Mr. Spencer must have been!'

'Oh, he's not dead yet!'

'Get away! He's been dead more than five thousand years.'

'Nonsense! He's writing his own life just now.'

'Well, now, that's funny. Do you know what year this is?'

'Yes; it's 1890.'

'It's nothing of the sort. It's 8020. See,' said the boy, showing Eaglesham the title-page of his book, 'there's the date—8020.'

'So it is! Where do you come from?'

'Nowhere. This is the world, isn't it?'

'Yes, but what country?'

'Country! Do you live in a country?'

'Yes; in Scotland, the northern part of Great Britain.'

'How funny! I'm reading about Great Britain here. Since my father wrote the observation quoted by Mr. Spencer, we have learned much more about the prehistoric ages. Manuscripts, and books, and lots of things have been found, preserved deep down in the glacial strata; and this is a boy's book telling a story founded on information obtained from these old writings.'

'Most extraordinary!'

'Isn't it! Here are you living in 1890; and here's me living in 8020, talking together in the office of Messrs. Clay, Clod, and McLatchy. I wonder how I came here.'

'So do I,' said Eaglesham.

'I suppose I'll go away just as I came.'

'I suppose so.'

'It's a very interesting book this. Would you like to hear some of it?'

'I would indeed.'

'I'll read you a bit of it, then.'

The boy turned back to the beginning of his book, saying: 'You must know that this is the story of the first historical boy. There is a preliminary chapter which shows who and what were the English, his ancestors. It explains what it was that first started the atmospheric and other changes which gradually reduced the inhabitants of the world to two—the human inhabitants, you know—one, a little boy, who wakened up one morning at the North Pole, to find himself, as he thought, alone in the world; and the other, a little girl, who wakened up on the same morning at the South Pole with the same thought. The story is how these two found each other after stupendous adventures. Now, I'll read you the preliminary chapter, and I think you'll find it very interesting.'

The little boy cleared his throat, and read what follows—viz., the first chapter of the historical romance entitled 'The First Boy.'

'Our knowledge of the history and geography of the world as it was before our era, even my youngest reader may remember is still in its infancy. We know most about a portion of land which belonged to our forefathers, and lay in what was termed the North Temperate Zone. It was called Britain, and seems to have been an island. The inhabitants were called English.

'The human inhabitants of the earth were not then one race, speaking one language. They were divided into many species, each species having a different dress, a different language, and a separate territory, the boundaries of the last being a constant source of dispute. Some of my young readers may remember the shudder which passed over the whole world one morning when the press announced authentically, that our predecessors in this globe had for thousands of years habitually settled the most trifling disputes by what they called *War*. We have been able to make out from certain of their writings that these people never themselves realised to the full the horrors of this devilish art—for it became an art, and had professors who lived by it alone. It cannot, therefore, be possible for us to comprehend in any due degree the misery brought about by its practice. According to its success in *War* was a people great. Now the English were the greatest warriors, and consequently the greatest and most enlightened people, in the world for many hundreds of years. From our knowledge of their manners and customs this fact tells us in what a terribly savage state the other peoples must have been, especially a race called the French, who were the neighbours of the English, but, from certain statements in the writings of the latter, a people most unlike them in all good qualities.

Many of the manners and customs of the English are inexplicable. For example, the name of one of their great institutions, *Rich-and-Poor*, conveys no meaning to us. One feature, however, a very expert ethnologist has been able to make out. By its establishment all people were divided into two classes or castes, viz.: those who had nothing to do, and had all the good things of life at their disposal; and those who had all the work to do, and in return received, very grudgingly from the others, food and time to sleep. Sometimes I think that this must have been a much worse institution even than *War*. Traces are not wanting in the writings of those unfortunate people of an inclination to rebel against this institution; but, as one of their thinkers said, they were enchanted, and could only submit.

'There seems to have been a time when Britain lost its supremacy. The chief cause of this period of eclipse, which was not of long duration, arose from injudicious treatment of the numerous colonies established by the English in various parts of the world. These offshoots were in some cases allowed to straggle pretty much as they pleased; in others, trained in a manner contrary to their actual bent; in all mismanaged. Britain, a small over-populated island, was no longer able to cope single-handed with any of the powerful peoples of Europe—the name of the large territory inhabited by the French, Germans, and Russians. These nations, all of them related by blood and language to the English, had for centuries been at war among themselves. But there had grown up an incontrollable hatred of Britain. While the other nations had been wasting their energies in fighting each other, the English had amassed much more than their share of the world's wealth, and had acquired all the most valuable lands. Taking advantage of the estrangement of the English colonies from the mother-land, the nations of Europe formed an alliance for the overthrow of the British Empire. They combined their fleets, and sent two millions of men to invade the hated island. So great had been the breach between its colonies and Britain, that the Europeans did not think it necessary to take the former into account. Their whole power was concentrated against Britain; and, in spite of the opposition of the English fleet, until that time invincible, a landing was effected. For the first time during more than six hundred years a foreign army trod British soil. The captain of the British forces, unable to face such a mass of men in the open country, retired to London, the metropolis of the island. It is impossible for us to understand what London was; all we know is, that it was an immense place called a city, crowded with people.

'When the English army retreated to London it was followed by throngs of refugees from all parts of the country, until the city contained more than double its ordinary population. It was gorged with humanity, and the influx of the panic-stricken folk had to cease. A cordon of men—actual *soldiers*, as they called their professional fighters, could not be spared—soon surrounded the city, and there was an end to all ingress or egress except by order of the captain. An effective circumvallation was rapidly improvised, and the siege began.

'Contemporary accounts hitherto discovered are few, meagre, and contradictory; but we are able to give a short statement of the main features of the siege. There seems, first of all, to have been a pitched battle, in which the English were badly beaten, and driven behind their fortifications. Then the invaders began to throw explosives, killing many people and destroying many buildings. No attempt was made at first to fire the city, as the rank and file of the foreign armies would not hear of it, afraid lest too much of the expected loot might be destroyed.'

'By-the-bye,' exclaimed the boy, looking up from his book, 'I have skipped some foot notes, explaining words. I know their meanings, having read the chapter before. I suppose, as you are living about the time these events happened, you will know the meanings of all the words that are obsolete to us?'

'Perfectly,' said Eaglesham. 'Go on.'

The boy resumed his reading.

'But the European hordes grew impatient, and several quarters of the city were set on fire, the invaders anticipating that in the confusion they would be enabled to force an entrance. This ruse, however, failed, and the enemy withdrew to their trenches. A truce of several days was asked for and granted. The English rightly judged that the time was to be occupied in preparation for a general attack, and they set themselves to devise means to repel it. They had ammunition and explosives of extraordinary kinds, the nature and the employment of which are alike riddles to us. One of the numerous stratagems of the besieged we are enabled to describe. Between the city and the external fortifications there extended a belt varying from a hundred to a thousand yards. Many houses were in this space, but they were tenanted only by soldiers on duty. By a superhuman effort a great number of rails were laid across this zone, and all the available engines and railway-carriages, charged with explosives and missiles, were placed on them. On the expiry of the truce, as was expected, a furious onslaught began on all sides. Some resistance was made as a blind, but soon all the English withdrew behind the trains. With hideous clamour the enemy rushed like a boiling sea into the awful trap. Some hesitated for a moment, suspecting strategy, but the thought of the enormous wealth within their grasp urged them on. The trains were all ready; the electric wires all connected with a central battery. At once, at sixty miles an hour, some thousands of death-laden waggons ploughed through the appalled masses of men. In the preceding events of the siege close on half a million of the enemy had fallen; the remainder by this desperate stratagem was annihilated. We, who know death only as a cessation of life when the complement of years is ended, can but shudder and forget that such a doom was once fulfilled.

No shout of victory rose from the affrighted Londoners, nor were they allowed time to realise the success of their murderous device. While crowds were yet thronging to the barriers, the drums beat to arms, the bells hammered from all the steeples, and the people, with murmured wonder and questioning faces, surged into the streets and squares where their chief men dwelt. The news was soon published. A second army had been perceived by the balloon watchman marching from the north. A groan went through the whole city; shrieks and shouts and lamentations rose everywhere; but the order for all not under arms to retire to their houses was issued, and the streets were cleared for a breathing space—in some instances at the point of the bayonet.

'The second army, though not so well disciplined, outnumbered the first. Fully one-third of it consisted of barbarians from lands lying east of Europe. Their very dress was sufficient to strike terror to the hearts of less savage people; and they had strange music with them. The English army now suffered what it had often inflicted on others. In their own countries these barbarians had been defeated times without number by the English in *their* outlandish uniforms, with unknown music, and weapons apparently miraculous. But now the barbarians were the invaders, and the bulk of the English, panic-stricken, threw down their arms and fled. The unarmed populace was not slow to follow. The captain with a few hundred brave men surrounded one of their important buildings. We do not know of what nature this building was; but the captain judged rightly that the foreigners would not care to destroy it. By this disposition of his forces one point at least was gained: each man could die fighting with his back to the wall.

'The second army, after the stupor caused by the sight of the blackened, bloody, and still smoking belt of exploded humanity had in a measure passed, broke all bounds of discipline. " Revenge!" in one terrible roar and a hundred dialects carried new fear to the distant fliers; while the stern ring in the city gripped their weapons and knew their time had come. In groups, in fragments of regiment, in twos and threes, heedless of the word of command, the avengers rushed on. There was no pillaging; destruction reigned. Hundreds of people, belated by greed or foolhardiness, fell shrieking; street after street was set on fire, and for a time it seemed as if the whole city were about to perish. In vain the captains rode hither and thither, ordering and even slaying. What discipline could not do, the lust of spoil achieved. The immense wealth which lay to their hands had been forgotten in the first emotions of horror and vengeance; but blood and fire having taken the edge off these, and a sight of the treasure which was to be their principal pay having awakened a dread lest the prize should escape them, those who had taken the lead in destruction began to organise salvage parties, and in a short time most of the fires were under control.   Lust of pillage, however, proved as strong as that of vengeance ; discipline was further from reasserting itself than ever, and the leaders had given up in despair, when it was bruited about that a remnant of the British force still stood under arms.   On the spread of this news among the common soldiers the slumbering desire for vengeance woke up unsatiated, and a great body of them were soon in their ranks again.

'It was many hours since the last of the English had surrounded their famous building.   They could have fought, oh ! so well ! and died so manfully !   But they had not bargained for this waiting.   Every face was white, every eye bloodshot with anguish ; some fainted, and one man dropped dead.   Only the courage and endurance of their captain supported them.   He rode round at intervals with a word and a smile for every one.   They were at a considerable distance from the outskirts of the city, and during most part of their long vigil were utterly at a loss, except for the flames, as to what was going forward.   At last some idea of the disorderly state of the enemy dawned upon their leader, and a wild hope of defeating them piecemeal flashed through his brain ; but, while this was in contemplation, word came from the watchmen that a third army was approaching from the west.   Then the blood surged up into the faces of these men ; fire sprang from their eyes ; and, as if they had drunk deeply of strong wine, they shook off the drowsier hopelessness, and were clothed with defiant despair.   But word came that the standards of the new army were banners striped and starred; and with that a wail rose from the devoted ring, and strong men were convulsed with sobs. They knew by the banners that this army came from the United States—a country which had been their first great colony, but which, by their mismanagement, had broken from them altogether, and had latterly become a rival, though on moderately friendly terms. These banners told them that their very flesh and blood, speaking their own language, was come against them. They wept and cried aloud, and dashed themselves against the wall. It was not that their vanity was hurt; but that the sons of their great ancestors should come to rejoice in their final overthrow was more than they could bear.

'Suddenly shouts and a shot or two forced their tortured thoughts to a more pressing matter. The second army had found them out and were pouring upon them by every approach, the barbarians in the van. On they came, firing recklessly. Steady and true when actual damage could be done, the English replied, and the attacking party fell back. Twice again they came on, after delivering their fire, and twice again they were compelled to retire. The Europeans held aloof, having no intention of wasting their lives as long as a barbarian was left; and the leaders would not allow artillery, as they wished to save the buildings.

'The first three onslaughts had been carelessly conducted, or rather not at all conducted; a fourth was to be made with greater regularity. The word had just been given to advance, when there came a blast of music. All paused to listen. Though the players were at a distance, a blare of brass and roll of drums pealed forth unmistakably the tune of "Rule, Britannia," the war-song of the English. The barbarians were the first to recognise it. They had heard it on many a battle-field; and now, coming as it were out of the sky, it demoralised them and they fled precipitately. At first the English did not believe their ears; but as the tune grew louder and louder doubt fled. Nobody, however, except the leader, guessed what was taking place. He ordered his men to form in front of the building; then he said simply: "The Yankees."

'A flash of eyes like lightning glimmered over the forlorn troop, and a hoarse, hysterical cry burst from their quivering lips, followed by a stupendous cheer.

'"Follow me!" cried the captain.

'Shouting their war-song at the pitch of their voices, and with the tears streaming down their faces, they dashed through the amazed Europeans, and reached the Yankees without the loss of a single man.

'For weeks the United States forces had been in Britain, friendly from the first. A third European army, guarding the coast, had been fought with many times before they reached London. The moment the way was clear, they had advanced, playing the English war-song to announce their presence and their amity.

'In vain do we look for details of the events

succeeding the relief of London. The broad facts are these : the European armies had to surrender; all the English-speaking races united in a great federation; and there is no trace of the recurrence of a general war.

' One May morning a while after the close of the war, the English in Britain were taking a holiday. Peace, prosperity, and a considerable modification of the institution of *Rich-and-Poor* had improved the social condition in such a notable degree that some of the more sanguine were beginning to apply to their country the title, long disused, of " Merry England." In many places May-poles had been erected, and dancing and light-hearted festivity were going on in the open air, as in the times of their great poet Shakespeare—pretty much, from all that we can gather, in the manner of our own outdoor merry-makings.

' Without any warning, while the mirth was at its height, a long, hollow whisper was borne inward from the western sea-board—a whisper so deep and far-reaching that it was heard even at Lowestoftness, the most easterly point in Britain. A stagnation in the air as if the earth had stood still followed, and then a wind began. It came from the north-east, and was at first pleasant and bracing, for the sun shone in a cloudless sky. Gradually and then rapidly the cold increased; the heavens grew gray ; and snow began to fall. The ribbons were frozen to the May-poles ; the hobby-horse and the dragon's case, thrown aside by the horror-stricken Morris-dancers, made fantastic shapes under the snow ;

barrels of ale left running, froze at the tap with amber icicles. It is impossible to describe the terrors of that day and night. In twenty-four hours there was a change from the rosy blush and the green mantle of early summer to the nakedness and pallor of the depth of winter—such a winter as the country had never known, a winter that should last for ages. Britain was an iceberg. What had happened?

'The Nihilists, a party that wished for the overturn of all the institutions of their time in order to start afresh, had for many years been so silent that the world thought them entirely disorganised. This was not the case. Though silent they had not been idle. A large body of them, not known to be Nihilists, had secured territory on an isthmus which connected the two divisions of the western world. Their professed intention was to establish a colony which should govern itself on principles absolutely altruistic. The English, to whom the land belonged, surrendered gladly. Ship-loads of emigrants, all Nihilists, crossed from the eastern world; and no one interfered with the new attempt to realise the golden age.

'Now the ocean between the eastern and western worlds was an immense oval whirlpool, called the Atlantic, and the outside sweep of it was known as the Gulf-stream. This whirlpool brought round to Europe some of the warmth acquired by the waters as they span round the Tropics, and so maintained the equable climate of the North Temperate Zone.'

Suddenly the boy vanished. There was nothing but the grimy shadow on the wall. Ebenezer Eaglesham speculated for some minutes on the means adopted by the Nihilists to divert the course of the Gulf-Stream, for he thought that that must have been the way by which the change in the world's atmosphere had been wrought. He wondered if it could have been by an immense subterranean tunnel through Panama. Then he wondered what changes had followed which brought about the destruction of mankind, all except the hero and heroine of the story. Remembering, however, that the boy had been reading fiction to him, he concluded that it was not worth further consideration.

Staring vacantly, and with hasty yet curiously exact movements like those of a somnambulist, he put past his books and went home.

CHAPTER IX.

THE VERY TIMID GREAT MAN COMES OUT OF HIS SHELL.

'Very unscientific,' said Cosmo, after the applause which followed Ninian Jamieson's story had subsided. 'Very unscientific. Still, I think it's right in one point—in its method of bringing about a new order. I predict, gentlemen—mark me, I predict—that no change that is not infinitesimal will take place in the constitution of society except after some stupendous natural convulsion which shall extirpate, or almost extirpate, the race. I predict it, and I should like to carve it on the summit of Mount Everest or Kinchinjunga, and sign it " Cosmo Mortimer, *né* Hugh Smith," that coming ages might know how one man, at least, was not blinded by faddists and reformation-mongers, but understood that Nature alone could do what Nature intends. By-the-bye, that reminds me—— Here, Jamieson, take the chair. I'll be back in a little.'

Without another word, Cosmo Mortimer seized his hat and left the room.

'Isn't he an extraordinary man ?' said the secretary. 'You'll see he'll come back with something truly amazing. But take the chair, Mr. Jamieson ; take the chair.'

'Hear ! hear !' said the fifth Great Man in a very loud voice for him.

As Ninian took Cosmo's seat, the fifth Great Man remarked, still in a loud voice : 'I knew a punster once.'

It was evident that the fifth Great Man—the very timid Great Man—had something to say. He had been known once before, in the absence of Cosmo, to come out very strong, and probably he was going to distinguish himself again. His companions determined to help him. Each of them put his elbow on the table and turned his back on the very timid Great Man.

'I knew a punster once,' repeated the very timid Great Man ; but Ninian's eyes were fixed on him, and he couldn't get on. The honorary secretary whispered something to the deputy-chairman, who immediately threw his legs over one arm of his chair, and sat with his left side turned towards the very timid Great Man. Then the very timid Great Man came out of his shell.

'The punster's name was Peter Goram,' he said. 'Once he stopped me eagerly in the street. He was a woeful sight. His locks, which he wore long, and cut with his own hands in an irregular fashion, that he might be able to say—self-sacrificing genius !—" No barber would let such a shock of hair re-cross his threshold if he survived the shock of its entrance "—were tangled and frowsy. His moustache—the result of much labour, and which, in his lively moods, disported itself like a group of long-legged spiders pinned to his upper lip—hung flaccid, languid, broken-legged, and pale. He was so thin that there seemed no more flesh on his cheeks than served as paste to fasten the skin down. His eye-sockets were as deep and his eyes were as dingy-looking as coal-pits. I was appalled.

'"Goram," I cried, "what—what is the matter?"

'A lurid gleam shot up the shafts at the bottom of which his eyes, like black diamonds, lay imbedded; his trembling fingers hooked my button-hole, and with convulsive gulps he gasped: "McGlumpha! Oh McGlumpha! Three nights ago, at Thompsons', at a tea party, I could not speak a word. Galloway, the junior reporter of the *Chronicle*, was there. You know him. He is the lion of the Thompsons. They rejoice to think that he fills the lowest post on the reporting staff of the *Chronicle*. Oh, yes! They are perfectly well acquainted with, and glory in, the fact, that his dismissal has been imminent several times. They revel in the knowledge that his salary amounts to the sum of fifty pounds a year. They are proud of his friendship when they read the far-seeing political articles and the slashing reviews which he didn't write, and which they are perfectly confident he couldn't have written with three times his present supply of brains. They are!"

'"Goram, Goram, be calm," I interposed.

'"Hush!" he cried. "Let me go on. Miss Thompson indulges her taste for aërial architecture ou the stable foundation of the editor's failing health, and the perfectly groundless hope that Galloway will succeed him. Well, sir; well! This lion of the Thompsons has got a jackal : his jackal is his voice. He keeps it in the precincts of his stomach; and when he lets it out he seems unable to recall it. That jackal of his barked all night, except when there was dancing or singing. There were hardly six words spoken where I could not have slipped in a delightful pun; but it would have been throwing pearls before swine. For, once, when I made a little joke, and the table was about to break into a laugh, it beheld Galloway's unmoved visage, and resumed its gravity. The table would not smile unless its lion initiated. Fifty puns I coined that night I dared not utter. I have wandered about the city for three days, seeking for some one to receive them. If they were false florins people could not be shyer of them. Now, McGlumpha, old boy, you know what it is to suppress a sneeze or a yawn; but these acts of self-denial are nothing to the martyrdom of one who nips his own proper puns in the bud. It is like chopping one's finger off, or gouging one's eye out, or refraining to kiss a pretty girl whose mouth is all ready. In the course of the evening, fifty several times. two mouths — two words. I mean—approached each other, pouting for a pun; but I dared not sanction their union. McGlumpha, my dear old friend, you know me, and you will let me fire off these puns to you. I passionately desire to do so. I glow —I burn——"

'I whisked my button-hole from his finger and escaped. I learned afterwards that he stopped a policeman, an orange-woman, two news-boys, a railway-porter, and a sandwich man, who all gave him the slip, some of them rather roughly; and, finally, got rid of his puns to a blind beggar, whom he bribed to listen, and who improved the time by picking Goram's pockets.'

The very timid Great Man paused, and Jamieson was about to turn round, but the honorary secretary frowned and shook his head. No one else moved, no one spoke. Silently they smoked, and waited hopefully. They were not disappointed. The very timid Great Man began again.

'Many a man,' he said, folding his arms, and addressing a knot in the table, 'whom the world calls spendthrift is perhaps throwing his money about in sheer self-defence, knowing well his avaricious nature and desirous of begetting in himself a habit of liberality. I do not doubt it. Still less do I doubt that numberless unfortunate beings of the most diffident, gentle, and modest dispositions live and die martyrs to the world's false opinion of them. Shall I tell it? Shall I? Yes, I shall. I shall tell you,' still addressing the knot in the table, 'how I became so timid. Perpend! I, who am actually, and always was, the most modest of men, in the early part of my life acquired the reputation of being an impudent, overweening fool. At an early age—indeed, almost as soon as the consciousness of my own personality dawned upon me—I became aware of my exceeding modesty. I must have been a very precocious child, for a method of compensating for my virtuous failing immediately occurred to me. Like everything truly ingenious it was very simple. It consisted in relentlessly violating my nature by doing and saying the things from which I shrank. This principle I persistently applied for a number of years to the conduct of my life, with varying results.

'Imagine me in Perth, at the age of twenty-one, with a small property not fully let. I am an orphan. I make friends with a Mr. James Brydie, who has as much time on his hands as myself. We soon become inseparable. Brydie is a born confidant; I, a born confessor. He never tires of hearing me talk about myself and Jane Boyd, a lady whom I have loved from infancy. It is true Jane is not the belle of Pitshirra, my native village; but, according to my principle, which precludes me from loving a beautiful girl, I give myself up to adoring her. My modesty leads me to depreciate rather than to exalt my lady-love; but, true to my principle, I describe her to Brydie as a creature of the sweetest nature and most engaging appearance and manners. I lead him to understand that she loves me with a love surpassing anything in fiction. Although not consummately ugly nor wholly without common-sense, I know Jane to be the most common-place and common-looking girl in Pitshirra; yet I am so eloquent in praise of her physical and intellectual charms that Brydie will be satisfied with nothing but an introduction. Now, however remarkable it may appear, I am not personally known to the lady, though from sundry mystic revelations in ecstatic moments I am sometimes persuaded that my love is returned. I shrink at first, as may be imagined, from taking Brydie to visit Jane. Still, such an opportunity of overcoming my modesty is not likely to occur again, and I determine to satisfy my friend.

'Pitshirra is within easy walking distance of Perth. On a Saturday afternoon we take the road thither. My friend seems to have picked up the notion that I am well acquainted with Miss Boyd—probably from my talk, although I have never affirmed it. I burn to tell him how ideal our relation is ; but, of course, dare not. I therefore keep up the deception ; and to prepare him for an exceedingly possible coldness of manner on Miss Boyd's part, I say to him as we jog along, "Jane is in some respects a very peculiar girl. I believe she would make a splendid actress. One never knows what mood she may be in, nor to what length she may carry any absurd notion that may strike her. For example : she sometimes takes it into her head not to know me, to look upon me as an impertinent intruder, and to shut the door in my face. And she does this in a manner so natural that a stranger would imagine she was in earnest."

'"But surely," says Brydie, "she doesn't treat you in this way before strangers?"

'"Doesn't she though! Just wait till you see. I

shouldn't wonder, now, if she affronts me in a scandalous manner to-day."

' "Well, I hope not," says Brydie.   "You told her I was coming?"

' "Of course, my dear fellow.   And I assured her you were my best friend.   But, don't you see, she will feel herself all the more at liberty to be fantastic on that account."

' "Ah! so she will," says Brydie.   "Well, if she insults us, I'll horsewhip you, seeing I can't strike a woman."

' "This is most unexpected—most unexpected, to say the least—Mr. Brydie.   I thought we were friends."

' "Why, so we are; but I tell you, McGlumpha, I never was insulted yet without taking it out of somebody.   Your back will suffer, sir, if Miss Boyd doesn't know you."

'I quiver all over to spring at his throat, and throw him down, and trample on him.   I never was nearer breaking my rule in my life.   With a great effort I conquer my modesty, and propose to defer our visit; but Brydie won't hear of it.

'When we arrive at Miss Boyd's garden-gate I think of a plan for avoiding any serious misunderstanding with Brydie.

' "Ha!" I cry.   "Do you see that striped blind in one of the upper windows, half-down and twisted?"

' "Yes; what of it?"

' "That's the sign that Jane's not at home."

' " Is it ? Perhaps it's only one of her tricks."

' " No. That's *bonâ fide*."

' " Look here, McGlumpha," says Brydie, suddenly ; " do you know Miss Boyd ?"

' " Know Jane ! Why ?——here she comes ! "

' The house-door opens, and the lady in question —much to my astonishment—trips down the garden walk. She seizes me with both hands, and says, " Hillo, Alistair ! Hoo are ye the day ? An' this is your freen' ? Ye're verra walcome, sir, for Alistair's sake."

' I can hardly contain myself. Still, I have enough presence of mind to whisper to Brydie, as we walk up to the house, " She's going to do the Scotch peasant-girl to-night. Isn't she splendid ?"

' When we were seated in the parlour, Miss Boyd says, " Weel, Alistair, an' hoo's yer bit proaperty dacin' ? Is't a' let yet ?"

' " No, Jane," with a gulp.

' " Mon, but that's a peety. I'm gettin' tired waitin' on ye."

' This is confounding, but I keep it up.

' " Jane, dear," biting my tongue, " remember Mr. Brydie's present."

' " An' what although ? He's only a callan, like yersel'."

' " Miss Boyd," says Brydie, " I own to being a callan, but surely not one like Mr. McGlumpha."

' " Weel, there's waur-lookin' fallows than Alistair,

mind ye," says Miss Boyd, "though, mebbe, no' mony.'

' "Jane, Jane!" I cry, shaking my head, "you're a dreadful girl."

' "This is intolerable," cries Brydie. " Can't you, or won't you, see through it ? You wretched puppie ! I am Miss Boyd's cousin."

' " Yes, Mr. McGlumpha," says the lady, rising, "and you have to thank me that you escape a well-merited whipping. I persuaded my cousin that this little farce would be a sufficient punishment, as, I trust —although Mr. Brydie does not—that you have some kind of conscience."

' Before I can reply, they leave the room. I question very much if they would have understood the Dante-Beatriceque nature of my love. Gentlemen, I have told you. That blighted me. I ceased to struggle against my unfortunate disposition, and gradually sank from modesty to bashfulness, and from bashfulness to timidity. It is only the meetings of this club that prevent me from falling from timidity into idiocy.'

Hardly was the last word out of the very timid great man's mouth, when Cosmo Mortimer returned. At once Ninian Jamieson resumed his own seat, and Cosmo took the chair of honour.

' Mr. President,' said the secretary, rising, ' before anything further is done it is necessary to drink the health of McGlumpha. On the last occasion when

McGlumpha spoke we drank his health specially. That is two years ago. McGlumpha has spoken again. The health of McGlumpha!'

'Certainly,' said Cosmo. 'I congratulate Mc Glumpha on his success. If McGlumpha ever succeeds in speaking more than three or four sentences in my presence I will make him president of this club for a year.'

McGlumpha sighed, shook his head, and stared at the knot in the table.

'Gentlemen,' resumed Cosmo, 'I have found them.' And he shook out a small bunch of manuscript. 'It flashed upon me in a moment, after Mr. Jamieson had finished, that I had a story to cap his. It is years since these papers came into my hands, but I am not at liberty to give any account of them. Fill your glasses, gentlemen, as it's a long story. I call it "The Salvation of Nature." I'm not going to read it; but I require to refer to some documents here, as there are facts and figures to deal with. I shall, like the honorary secretary, plunge *in medias res.*

CHAPTER X.

THE SALVATION OF NATURE.

On the day that Sir Wenyeve Westaway's World's Pleasance Bill became law, the happy baronet kissed his wife and said, 'Lily, darling, it has taken twenty years, but we have saved Nature.'

'Never mind, dear,' said Lady Westaway, who, though a true helpmeet, loved to quiz her husband; 'the time has not been wholly wasted.'

'Wholly wasted!' cried Sir Wenyeve, too much in earnest for even the mildest *persiflage*. 'The salvation of Nature is a task worthy of an antediluvian lifetime.'

'In the longest life there is only one youth,' sighed Lady Westaway, as she left the library.

She was thirty-five years old, and her married life had been a continuous intrigue to bring about the fulfilment of her husband's dream. Now that his object was gained, she felt that her youth and prime had passed like a rout at the close of the season—stale, unenjoyed, immemorable. But she dressed beautifully on the night of her husband's triumph; and the subtler of her guests mistook the sadness in her eyes and voice for the exquisite melancholy which overcomes some natures when an arduous undertaking is accomplished.

The day after Sir Wenyeve's banquet celebrating the passage of his Bill, two thousand clerks and message-boys posted two million copies of the following prospectus. The list of directors, financial agents, bankers, managers, and other uninteresting details are omitted.

THE WORLD'S PLEASANCE COMPANY (LIMITED).

Incorporated under the Companies Acts.

Capital . . . 200,000,000*l.*

Issue of 1,000,000 shares of 100*l.* each, of which 50*l.* is called up as follows :—5*l.* on application, 5*l.* on allotment, 20*l.* on May 1, and 20*l.* on July 1. The remaining 50*l.* per share is to form security for debentures.

The capital of the company is divided into 2,000,000 shares of 100*l.* each, of which—

1,650,000 shares will be issued as ordinary shares, entitled to a cumulative dividend of 15 per cent. before the deferred shares participate in profit.

350,000 shares as deferred shares to be issued at 50*l.* paid, which will not be entitled to participate in dividend until 15 per cent. has been paid on the paid-up capital of the ordinary shareholders.

The deferred shares and 600,000 of the ordinary shares will be taken by the promoters in part payment of the price.

This company has been incorporated for the purpose of acquiring that part of Great Britain known as the kingdom of Scotland, with the outer and inner Hebrides and the Orkney and Shetland Isles.

It is estimated that three-quarters of the capital of the company will be expended on the purchase of Scotland; the remainder to be devoted—

1. To the demolition of all manufactories, foundries, building-yards, railways, tramways, walls, fences, and all unnatural divisions, and of all buildings, with some few exceptions, of a later date than 1700 A.D.

2. To the purchase of a number of the Polynesian Islands.

3. To the importation of these islands and the distribution of their soil over the razed cities, towns, villages, etc.

When the land has thus been returned to the bosom of Nature, it will remain there unmolested for a year or two. At the end of this nursing-time, Scotland, having been in a manner born again, will be called by its new name 'The World's Pleasance'; and visitors will be admitted during the six months of summer and autumn on payment of 50*l.* for each individual per month. At the rate of 100,000 visitors per month, this will give an income of 30,000,000*l.* Figures like these need no comment.

Every species of tent, marquee, awning, and canvas or waterproof erection; every species of rowing or sailing vessel; and every species of rational land conveyance will be permitted in the World's Pleasance: but there must not be laid one stone upon another; nor shall steam, electricity, or hydraulic power be used for any purpose, except for the working of Professor Penpergwyn's dew-condensers. One of these machines will be erected at John o' Groat's House, and another at Kirkmaiden. Professor Penpergwyn has recently, at the request of the promoters of this company, devoted all his time to perfecting his celebrated apparatus; and we are happy to be able to state that the cloud-compelling attachment for withholding rain from an area greater than half that of Scotland, now works with the requisite power, regularity, and delicacy; while the dew-condensers proper can, at a moment's notice, fill the air with any degree of moisture, from the filmiest mist to a deluge.

The promoters of this company congratulate themselves, and the peoples of every continent, on the salvation of a fragment of the Old World from the jaws of Civilisation; and in conclusion they think they cannot do better than quote the peroration of Sir Wenyeve Westaway's great speech on the motion for the third reading of the Bill with which his name will be associated to the end of time. The honourable baronet said in conclusion, 'If you would loosen the shackles which bind the poetry and art of the day; if you would give a little ease to the voiceless, suffering earth, crushed in the iron shell of civilisation, like the skull of a martyr in that Venetian head-screw which ground to a pulp bone and brain and flesh; if, in a word, you would provide a home, a second Academe, a new Arcadia for poetry and art, these illustrious outcasts; if you would save Nature, you will pass this Bill. Make Scotland the World's Pleasance, and I venture to predict that the benefits springing from such a recreation-ground to Art and Morality will be so immense, that the world will bless, as long as the earth endures, the legislators who licensed the creation of a second Eden.'

The demand for shares during the week in which the prospectus was published was more than double the supply. Ling-long, the Chinese perpetual president of the United States, applied for a thousand; but his Perpetuity had to be contented with ten. All the kings and queens in the world took as many as could be allotted to them. The ancient list of the world's seven wonders was cancelled, and the company's palatial and labyrinthine offices on the English banks of the Tweed became the initial wonder of a new one. And Sir Wenyeve Westaway? He was made a peer of the realm, and the company, in the joy of success, voted him for two lives the sole right of visiting the island of Arran.

Professor Penpergwyn superintended the destruction of civilised Scotland. Electrite was the explosive used, on account of the precision with which the upheaval produced by a given charge could be calculated. It was possible with this remarkable invention to destroy one half of a building, and leave the other undamaged; for the *débris* fell back, like an ill-thrown boomerang, exactly to the spot whence it had shot up. The Professor was truly a great man. When all the railways and tramways had been removed, and sold at great profit to the Chinese; when all the wires had been prepared, and half the known tar, and every tar-barrel beneath the sun had been duly distributed among the buildings to be deracinated, he let the world into the secret of the broad and lofty piers which he had erected on many parts of the Scottish coast, at various distances from the shore. From them the public could view the great fire, on payment to the Professor of three guineas per head. He provided no conveyance to or from the piers. He guaranteed nothing, either regarding their security or the width of view which they commanded. You paid your money and took your chance. Two million people bought tickets. The Professor's profit, deducting the cost of the piers, and of the huge army of ticket-collectors, was 2,000,000*l.*

On the last night of the year, Scotland was set on fire. The Professor had utilised the Scotch telegraph wires. By their means all his mines were connected with the battery at which he sat in London, waiting impatiently till ten should strike. In the moment of the last stroke he touched the machine; then he set off for Kamtschatka with his wife and his only daughter, a child of seven years.

As will be surmised, this extraordinary man was

not the only individual who waited with impatience till
ten o'clock that night. All England, all the world was
en fête. Miniature explosions were prepared in every
town and hamlet, in nearly every street and lane in the
four quarters of the globe—each little mine surrounded
by a restless mob. But the most impatient of all the
inhabitants of the earth were the two millions of men
and women who crowded the Professor's piers.

At a minute from ten, the human zone girdling
Scotland was as silent as death. All the clocks in all
the towers and steeples in the doomed country had
been wound up for that night. There was no wind,
and the air was frosty. When the hour rang—the last
hour that should ever ring in Scotland—pealing in
many tones, but harmonised by the distance to the ears
of the listeners, so that poets thought of swan-songs
and the Phœnix, and the most prosaic remembered the
death-knell—a strong thrill passed through the multi-
tude, and a rustle went about from pier to pier, like a
wind wandering among the woods. Not a star could
be seen. Scotland was only discerned as a more intense
blackness in the bosom of the night. The silence after
the striking of the hour was deeper than before—so
deep that the people heard faintly the petty plash of
the waves against the piers.

Suddenly the Cheviots were tipped with fire, and
two million faces grew pale. In the same breathless
instant these faces, rank after rank, loomed out in the
light of the burning country, as the land-wide flash

sped over the mountains to Cape Wrath, and a sound as if the thunder of a century had been gathered into one terrific long-rolling peal, shook the whole sea, and forced every head to bend. Then again silence and blackness, uttermost, appalling. All the people trembled. A wife said to her husband in the lowest whisper ever breathed, 'I am going mad.'

'And I too,' he replied hoarsely.

A sage old man beside them, who overheard their whispers, cried 'Hurrah!'

It broke the spell. From pier to pier the word ran until the shout became general.

'Hurrah! hurrah!'—the most voluminous cheer on record—and with that the people fell a-talking.

'Has it failed?' was the universal question. The wise old fellow who had started the cheer thought not.

'The explosions are over,' he said, 'but the fires will soon break out.'

And he was right. Even as he spoke tongues of flame were jetting up. It was then five minutes past ten. In another minute, Scotland looked like a huge leviathan, spotted and brindled with eyes and stripes of fire. Where the towns were thick these ran into each other, and soon the Lowlands were wrapped in one glowing sheet. The smoke wallowed on high, and dipped and writhed in and out among the flames. Description shrivels before such a scene.

'Behold,' cried Lord Westaway, 'the altar on which

the world sacrifices to Nature for the sin of Civilisation !'

It is not known when the last flame of the great fire went out ; but in the end of February the first fleet of vessels from Polynesia arrived in the Clyde. They landed their cargoes among the ruins of Glasgow ; and the *débris* on the Broomielaw was soon covered with the dust of the coral insect.

In six months the reclamation of Scotland to the bosom of Nature was completed by a million men, who wrought in three relays, night and day. Professor Penpergwyn's piers were then destroyed ; and a cordon of five hundred war-vessels was placed along the coast, and not a human foot trod Scottish earth—or Polynesian earth in Scotland—for two years.

Lord Westaway, on the day the company granted him the Island of Arran, had shut himself up in his study. Three hours he brooded, and then summoned his son, Lewellyn, a handsome boy in his eleventh year.

'Lewellyn,' said Lord Westaway, 'I am going to prepare Arran for you. You will enter into possession on your twenty-first birthday. I will make it the most remarkable island in the world.'

'How will you do that, papa ?'

'Do not inquire ; don't try to discover from any source : your surprise and pleasure ten years hence will be the greater.'

The boy, who worshipped his father, agreed to this unhesitatingly.

The World's Pleasance brought down the world. At the close of the first season in which the rejuvenated Scotland was open to the public, instead of the fifteen per cent. expected by the promoters, a dividend of thirty per cent. was declared on all the shares. From many glowing contemporary accounts of the wonders of the great pleasure-ground, I select the following letter of the young Empress of the East to her Prime Minister, whom she afterwards married, as being the least over-charged :—

Extract from the letter of the Empress of the East.

We landed in the end of June on the shore where Leith once stood. I was carried up to Edinburgh in a litter, the rugged nature of the ground preventing any other mode of conveyance. A Greek temple-like build-ing—formerly a picture-gallery, I believe—had been prepared for us. The rent of it is enormous, as the company put up to auction all the habitable buildings in the country. This was rendered necessary by the battles which took place for the possession of historical or finely situated houses. At first the directors thought the fighting would lend an additional charm to life here ; but when Ling-long, the American president, besieged the Emperor of the French in Holyrood with bows and arrows and battering-rams—a bye-law forbids the use of all explosives—and took the palace with the loss of several lives on both sides, interference was deemed expedient. All fighting, except in the tourney, is now done with quarter-staves. Every third day we have a quarrel with some other potentate about a fishing-stream or a glade for hawking in. My greatest enemy is the King of England, who lives in Edinburgh Castle. We are very warm friends and model disputants, complying graciously with the bye-law, which adjudges victory to the side that first draws blood. Although the King's retinue exceeds mine, my Tartar giant, by his superior strength and agility, manages, as a rule, to finish the fight in our favour.

'I will just go on scribbling in my woman's way as I have begun. The next thing that occurs to me is the splendour of Edinburgh. It is pronounced by everybody the most beautiful piece of the juvenile country. Scientific men are much perplexed by it, as indeed they are by all the newly naturalised land. It would seem that at present there is a struggle going on between the imported tropical vegetation and the native plants and grasses. The latter have conquered in Edinburgh. It is covered with young heather and broom and bracken, and only here and there a dwarfed alien plant appears. The billows of purple and green and gold toss about in what was the New Town, and, swirling across the valley, roll up the High Street to throw splashes of colour here and there on the Castle esplanade.

'We are clad in sixteenth century costumes; the King of England and his Court in dresses of the time of the Charleses. Nearly all the Americans go about in Greek robes, as gods and goddesses, heroes and heroines. The French Court is a miniature of that of Louis XIV. The Russians are dressed in Lincoln green; the Czar is called Robin Hood, and the Czarina, Maid Marian. We have no clocks; the dial is our only time-keeper. It is all a great masque, from the country itself to the pot-boys and scullions. Last week I rode as far north as Perth, and seemed to journey through all the times and peoples of Europe. Here, in a broad meadow, we saw a tournament, where some princess sat as queen of love and beauty. A few miles further on we passed a water-party of the Restoration, with music and laughter. Then a pavilion gleamed white among the trees, and there two knights of the Round Table hung out their blazoned shields. Up rode, with lofty air, Don Quixote, wearing the veritable helmet of Mam-brino. Behind, all amort, on a sorry ass, ambled the wisest of fools, dear old Sancho Panza. "What, ho! vile recreants!" cried the knight of La Mancha, and struck exultingly one of the shields. We stood aside to watch the encounter, and beheld him of the sorrowful counten-ance go down before the spear of Launcelot of the Lake. Anon, Mary, Queen of Scots, followed by Douglases and Graemes and Setons, sped by, chasing a stag of ten. "Splenderr de Dieu!" cried a deep voice in front; and a body of Norman knights charged the Scotsmen. But after a brief battle, William the Conqueror and Mary Stuart agreed to hunt together.

'O me! my heart is sick with dreaming over these

old times! And yet, although I know it is the signal for my return, I long for the day when you are to come, my faithful friend.

'I have some, and shall have more, very pleasant stories to tell you of a party of Germans, who have undertaken to act through all Shakespeare's comedies, with the whole World's Pleasance for stage, naming places after localities in the plays, and travelling about as the scene requires. They have already acted two comedies, and in each of them real passions and events have grown out of the fiction, so that the company has lost half its original members owing to elopements and quarrels. This is a long letter, and I am tired.'

One result of the success of the World's Pleasance Company was the establishment of similar companies in nearly every country. The Americans reclaimed Peru and California. The Empress of the East was the principal promoter of a company for the naturalisation of Greece. The French reclaimed Provence; the Germans the Rhine Provinces. Italy was given over entirely to nature; and the whole Italian nation became brigands. This country was much frequented by young people in search of adventure. The African Republics made pleasances of Algeria, and the country about the great lakes; and a gigantic Asiatic company bought up the Himalayas and the Indo-Chinese Peninsula. For eight years all these pleasance companies paid great percentages, and immense fortunes were made. Every other man was a millionaire. Then it seemed that the world came bankrupt. Thousands of people committed suicide. Famine followed bankruptcy; and after it came a new disease. It began in India, and travelled almost as fast as the news of its ravages. People fled to their pleasances for refuge, but the pest was there before them. Cities were emptied in a day. In every town and hamlet the last to die thought himself the last man, and posed mentally as such. London was swept of life like the deck of a vessel by a mountainous wave. In the World's Pleasance people wandered about in twos and threes, shunning strangers, digging roots, dropping dead. Most of them wore their holiday costumes. Some few carried bottles of wine, and laughed and sang. But the time for such desperate jollity soon passed, and the plague remained.

In the beginning of July, an old man of great freshness and vigour appeared in that part of the Pleasance formerly known as Ayrshire. He approached everybody he met. To those whom he could stay, he put this question, 'Do you know anything of Lewellyn Westaway?' A languid shake of the head was all the answer he ever got. So many kept him aloof, that he resorted to calling out his question at the pitch of his voice. For an entire forenoon he did this; and shortly after midday a man dropped out of a tree almost on his head, and said, 'I am Lewellyn Westaway.'

'And I,' said the old man, 'am Professor Penpergwyn.'

The Professor wore a white hat and a black frock coat, old and rusty. Lewellyn was dressed in a purple velvet doublet, and from his close-fitting cap a feather hung gracefully, and mingled with his long hair. The contrast was striking.

'What do you want with me?' asked Lewellyn.

'Why are you not in Arran?'

'In Arran?'

'Yes; you are twenty-one now, and the island awaits you.'

'I had forgotten about it.'

'Drink this, and go there at once.'

'What's this? and why should I go there at once?'

'This,' said the Professor, opening the morocco-case he had offered Lewellyn, and holding up a little vial, 'is an infallible remedy for the plague.'

Lewellyn laughed scornfully.

'Faithless, faithless!' cried the Professor, looking earnestly with his strong convincing eyes into those of the young man.

Lewellyn was bound by his gaze; and the Professor continued: 'I tell you, who may die this moment, who must die within a week, that this will save you, and you laugh in my face. Will you take it or not?'

Lewellyn took it.

'Drink it.'

He did so in silence.

'Now listen to me.'

The Professor leaned against a tree, while Lewellyn stood meekly before him.

' First tell me : are your father and mother dead ? '

' They are.'

' Then you are as free as I could wish you to be, unless you are married.'

' I am not.'

' Good. Many years ago I discovered this disease in Kamtschatka. It is really nothing more or less than hunger, the millionth power of hunger. I have not time to explain it. It must often have appeared in the world. Probably it has always existed actively, but never till this great famine has it fairly got wing. I recognised its power in Kamtschatka, and saw that if it should get strength from feeding on a few thousand lives, it would kill the world. Its power and velocity increase with its progress. It knows no crisis. In a few days it will be as swift as the lightning. I began in Kamtschatka to try for a remedy. I laboured for years, and then had to come west for materials. It was during that visit that I burned Scotland. On my return to Kamtschatka I found that a filtrate I had left standing had clarified itself, and was, in fact, the required remedy. For the last ten years I have been trying to repeat the process, but have always failed. When I heard of the breaking out of the pest I came at once from Kamtschatka. I had sufficient of my remedy to save two lives. My wife is dead, so I give one half to you. Now, sir, go to Arran.'

'Why give me half?'

'Is that your gratitude? Had I not found you I would have given it to the finest young fellow I could meet with. But ask no more questions. Do as I bid you. You will find it to your advantage. You will never see me more. Within a fortnight all who have not drunk of my medicine will be dead.'

'What! Are we two to be the only men left alive, and are we to part for ever?'

'Yes. Your father has saved Nature, but in a way he little expected. Good-bye for ever.'

Lewellyn realised but faintly what the old man had said with such authority, and stood irresolute.

'Go,' said the Professor, and Lewellyn, like one under a spell, hurried down to the coast. He was hardly out of sight when Professor Penpergwyn dropped dead.

On the shore Lewellyn found many boats—some floating, some high and dry—all masterless. He chose the one he judged the swiftest sailer, and was soon flying across the firth with a strong east wind behind him. As he neared Arran he saw a white flag run up a short pole on a little eminence near the beach. He was too much battered with wonder to feel this new stroke. Involuntarily he steered for the flag. When he was some hundred yards from land he observed below the flag-pole, seated on a rock, a figure like that of a woman, motionless and watching him intently. In landing, his boat occupied all his attention, so that when he stepped ashore and found a tall girl standing with her back to him, but within reach of his arm, the effect upon him was almost as great as if he had not seen her before. He stood still, expecting her to turn round; but she remained as she was for some moments, fingering a bow she carried. A quiver full of arrows was slung across her shoulder. Her dress of some dark blue homely stuff came to her ankles. She wore shoes of untanned leather, and a belt of the same in which was stuck a short sword. On her head she had a little fur cap, and her short golden brown hair curled on her shoulders. Slowly she turned and gave him a side glance. Then she looked him full in the face and sighed deeply, but as if some doubt had been resolved to her satisfaction. He fell back a step at the splendour of her eyes. Her face was broad and her complexion delicate, though browned. He hardly noticed her low forehead, her straight eyebrows, her strong, round chin, and full red mouth; her eyes held him. He did not think of their colour. He was subdued by their intense expression. They seemed to pierce him with intuition, and at the same time to bathe him in a soft, warm light. She spoke, and her voice seemed to caress him; but all she said was 'Do you come from Professor Penpergwyn?'

He bowed. If he spoke he felt the vision would vanish.

'Have you drunk the other half?'

He bowed again, understanding her to mean the other half of the professor's remedy.

LYNI EN PENPERGWYN WATCHING LEWELLYN

' Did he tell you there was only enough for two?'

He found his tongue and answered ' Yes,' whispering as intensely as she did, but wondering why there should be so much passion about the matter.

' Do you know who drank the rest?'

' I supposed it was the Professor.'

She siged again, a deep sigh of satisfaction, and sank on the beach sobbing. Lewellyn, after a moment's thought, knelt beside her and held one of her hands in both his. She made no resistance. In a little she dried her tears with her disengaged hand, shook back her hair and looked him in the face.

' I'm so glad to see you,' she said, ' I have been alone here for a week. You needn't ask any questions. I'll tell you it all at once. Professor Penpergwyn is my papa. Is he alive?'

' He was four hours ago.'

' He may be dead now, though. Poor papa! He would always have his own way. Papa expected to find you. When he didn't he left me all alone and went to search for you. We brought some provisions and weapons with us, and I have managed to get on very well. But I'm glad you've come. *Are* you Lewellyn Westaway?' she cried sharply, springing to her feet in sudden doubt.

' Yes, I am—Lord Westaway, if it's of any consequence.'

' I'm very glad. Tell me what was the name of your father's steward.'

' Dealtry—Henry Dealtry ? '

' It was ; it was ! '

The lady smiled, and looked as happy and self-satisfied as if she had exercised the most extra-ordinary subtlety in putting this question, and as if Lewellyn's answer were conclusive proof of his identity.

' But you must be hungry,' she said suddenly. ' Come.'

She led him to a tent at the entrance of a little glen, and bade him sit on the turf at the door, while she went in. A pleasant odour came through the canvas, and he heard the clatter of dishes—a very wholesome sound to one who had been living a half-savage life for several weeks.

Soon she cried ' Come in,' and he entered.

' I began to prepare this little dinner when I saw your boat far, far away.'

He thanked her and they ate in silence, stealing shy glances at each other, and feeling a little uncomfortable. But being hungry they did not mind that much.

' Now,' she said, resuming her frankness, not perfectly however, ' if you're quite satisfied, come and I'll show you the wonders of your island. You know your father promised you it should be the most remarkable island in the world.'

' And so it is,' he said, looking at her steadily.

She blushed, and said nothing.

They had not taken many steps up the glen when
a roar shook the ground.

He stopped in wonder. She answered the question
in his eyes.

'That's the old lion. He's the only one left.'

'The only one!'

'Are you frightened? He's not at all dangerous
He's got hardly any teeth, and he just crawls. I'll tell
you all about it now, although I meant to show it to
you before explaining. My father and I met Dealtry,
your father's steward, in London, and he told us about
the island being yours, and how your father promised
you it should be the most remarkable island in the
world, and how in fulfilment of that promise he stocked
it with all kinds of wild beasts and birds and insects,
intending it to be a great hunting-ground. Dealtry
told us you would be sure to be here.'

'I had forgotten all about it.'

'Well, except this old lion, all the originals are
dead. But there are many elephants, lions, tigers,
bears, leopards, hyenas, and beasts I don't know the
names of—all very little, and not at all fierce. They're
fast dying out too, for they can't get any food. You'll
hardly see a deer, and even rabbits are scarce. There's
a tiger!'

Lewellyn saw a striped beast about the size of a
Newfoundland dog slinking across the path before them.
While he looked at it curiously, something whistled
through the air, and with a scream the beast rolled

over, pierced to the heart by one of Miss Penpergwyn's arrows.

'I always shoot them,' she said, 'and you will do so, too; for we must get rid of them. That was papa's order.'

Lewellyn sighed, and thought of *his* father. This was the end of his high-pitched imaginings, and passionate endeavours to realise what others would never dream of imagining. A melancholy, profounder than that which was normal to all high-strung souls at that dread time, seized him and was reflected by his companion. They wandered about the island, hand in hand, saying little. Every foreign beast, bird, and insect that they saw, all small, and much less brilliant than in their native climes, increased his melancholy until it became almost an agony, and he was glad when they reached the tent again. She bade him sit once more at the entrance while she got supper ready.

'And while you are waiting,' she said, 'you can read this. My father left it for you, and I forgot about it till now.'

Lewellyn took from her a sealed letter, which he read slowly and with much emotion. He had been thinking over it for some minutes when he was summoned to supper.

'Come out,' he said.

Miss Penpergwyn obeyed.

'Stand beside me while I read this to you. There is no date. "You will be beginning to understand by this time. I had a long struggle with myself; but my life would soon have ended and hers was just beginning. I felt sure I would find you. I had known your father, and had seen you in your boyhood; I knew your character, and that you must be a strong and handsome man. The world begins again with you two." That is all. What is your name, Miss Penpergwyn?'

'Lynden.'

'Lynden! a strange name.'

'My father was a strange man.'

He took both her hands, and drew her towards him.

'Lynden Westaway,' he said.

She trembled; then, dropping her head on his shoulder, whispered between a sob and a laugh, 'My husband.'

.   .   .   .   .   .

Next morning Lewellyn said, 'I've been thinking over all you did yesterday, and there are two things I don't understand. Why did you sigh so deeply and gladly when I said I supposed your father had drunk the other half of the remedy?'

'Because I was glad that you hadn't taken it knowingly from him.'

'And why did you stand with your back to me when I landed, and then sigh so happily again when I turned round?'

I stood with my back to you because I was afraid

you might not be easy to love; and I sighed with happiness when I saw how handsome you were. Oh! how bold you must have thought me! I imagined that my father would have told you about me, and *all* he meant, and that was why I was so frank. I wanted to put you at your ease, my dear—to meet you half way, love.'

As soon as Cosmo had finished his extraordinary story the honorary secretary remarked in a deep voice: 'Gentlemän, it is now 3.30 A.M.'

'What!' cried Cosmo; 'and the whiskey not half done yet!'

He lifted the barrel. It felt very light. He shook it. There was no sound. He turned it up with the bung over his rummer. Not a drop came.

'Well,' said Cosmo, 'I'm damned! That's all—doubly and trebly. I thought it was only half done. . In that case there's nothing remains now but to break these rummers. No liquor less divine shall ever stain them.'

With that he flung his rummer into the empty fire-place, smashing it into a thousand pieces, and every man followed suit.

'"Auld Lang Syne,'" said Cosmo; and they sang it at the pitch of their voices.

'Secretary, do your duty,' said the President in his austerest tone.

'The suspension of Rule 6 is now cancelled, and

this extraordinary meeting of the Great Men at an end,' said the Secretary with precision.

The five Great Men then accompanied Ninian and Cosmo to the house of the latter, and, having cheered their President and their guest, went home quietly to their several places of abode.

NOTE

We are fortunate in being able to present the reader with the story referred to by Cosmo Mortimer. As we agree with him that the original title, 'The North Wall,' is ridiculous, we now call it 'A Practical Novelist.'

The question started by Cosmo as to the identity of the hero of 'A Practical Novelist' with Mr. Pourie is beyond our ability to solve. On the face of it, however, we are inclined to think they are different individuals; because, though it will be found that the morality of Mr. Maxwell Lee, the practical novelist, is even more peculiar than that of Mr. Pourie, it will also be found that it is a genuine morality, and not more properly to be described as immorality, which, we fear, must be the last word on Mr. Pourie's conduct.

CHAPTER I

BAGGING A HERO

'WELL, but the novel is played out, Carry. It has run to seed. Anybody can get the seed; anybody can sow it. If it goes on at this rate, novel-writers will soon be in a majority, and novel-reading will become a lucrative employment.'

'What are you going to do, then, Maxwell? Here's Peter out of work, and my stitching can't support three.'

The three in question were Maxwell Lee, his wife Caroline, and her brother, Peter Briscoe. Lee was an unsuccessful literary man; his brother-in-law, Briscoe, an unsuccessful business-man. Caroline, on the other hand, was entirely successful in an arduous endeavour to be a man, hoping and working for all three.

We have nothing whatever to do with the past of these people. We start with the conversation introduced in the first sentence. Caroline had urged on Lee the advisability of accepting an offer from the editor of a country weekly. But Lee, who had composed dramas and philosophical romances which no publisher, nor editor could be got to read, refused scornfully the task of writing 'an ordinary, vulgar, sentimental and sensational story of the kind required.'

'What am I going to do?' he said. 'I'll tell you: I am going to create a novel. Practical joking is the new novel in its infancy. The end of every thought is an action; and the centuries of written fiction must culminate in an age of acted fiction. We stand upon the threshold of that age, and I am destined to open the door.'

Caroline sighed, and Briscoe shot out his underlip: evidence that they were accustomed to this sort of thing.

Lee continued : 'You shall collaborate with me in the production of this novel. Think of it! Novel-writing is effete; novel-creation is about to begin. We shall cause a novel to take place in the world. We shall construct a plot; we shall select a hero; we shall enter into his life, and produce the series of events before determined on. Consider for a minute. We can do nothing else now. The last development, the naturalist school, is a mere copying, a bare photographing of life—at least, that is what it professes to be. This is not art. There can never be an art of novel-writing. But there can be—there shall be, you will aid me to begin the art of novel-creation.'

'Do you propose to make a living by it?' inquired Briscoe.

'Certainly.'

Briscoe rose, and without comment left the house.

Caroline looked at her husband with a glance of mingled pity and amusement.

'Why are you so fantastic?' she asked softly.

'You laugh at my idea now, because you do not see it as I see it. Wait till it is completely developed before you condemn it.'

Caroline made no reply; but went on with her sewing. Lee threw himself at full length on a rickety sofa and closed his eyes. Besides the sofa, two chairs and a table, a rag of carpet before the fire-place, a shelf with some books of poetry and novels, and an old oil-painting in a dark corner, made up the furniture of the room. There were three other apartments, a kitchen and two bedrooms, all as scantily furnished. The house was in the top flat of a four-storey land in Peyton Street, Glasgow.

Lee dozed and dreamed. Caroline sewed steadily. An hour elapsed without a word from either. Then both were aroused by the noisy entrance of Briscoe, who, having let himself into the house by his latch-key, strode into the parlour with a portmanteau in either hand. He thrashed these down on the floor with defiant emphasis, and said, frowning away a grin: 'Your twin-brother's traps, Lee. I'll bring *him* upstairs, too.'

He went out immediately, as if afraid of being recalled.

'Your twin-brother!' exclaimed Mrs. Lee. 'I never heard of him.'

'And I hear of him for the first time.'

They waited in amazement the return of Briscoe. Soon an irregular and shuffling tread sounded from the stair; and in a minute he and a cabman entered the parlour, bearing between them what seemed the lifeless body of a man. This they placed on the sofa. The cabman looked about him curiously; but, being apparently satisfied with his fare, withdrew.

When he was gone, Briscoe spoke: 'This is the first chapter of your novel, Lee. Something startling to begin with, eh?'

'What do you mean?'

'I've bagged a hero for you.'

'Bagged a hero!'

'Yes; kidnapped a millionaire in the middle of Glasgow in broad daylight. Here's how it happened: one instant I saw a man with his head out of a cab-window, shouting to the driver; the next, the cab-door, which can't have been properly fastened, sprang open, and the man was lying in the street. On going up to him, I said to myself, "Maxwell Lee, as I'm a sinner!" You're wonderfully like, even when I look at your faces alternately. Well, I shouted in his ear, "Chartres! Chartres!" seeing his name in his hat which had fallen off, and pretending to know him perfectly. I felt so mad at you and your absurd notions of creating novels, that, without thinking of the consequences, I got him into the cab again, told the policeman that he was my brother-in-law, and drove straight here. It was all done so suddenly, and I assumed such confidence, that the police did not so much as demand my address. Of course, if you don't want to have anything to do with him, I suppose we can make it out a case of mistaken identity.'

'Who is he, I wonder?' said Lee, whose eyes were sparkling.

'There's his name and address,' replied Briscoe, pointing to the portmanteaus.

Lee read aloud: '"Mr. Henry Chartres, Snell House, Gourock, N.B."' He then pressed his head in both hands, knit his brows, tightened his mouth, and regarded the floor for fully a minute.

As soon as Chartres had been laid on the sofa, Caroline wiped the mud from his face and hands. There was not a cushion in the room, but she brought two pillows from her own bed, and with them propped the head and shoulders of the unconscious man. While Lee was still contemplating the floor, she said, 'We must get a doctor at once.'

Lee's response was a muttered 'Yes, yes;' but the question brought him nearer the facts of the case than he had been since Briscoe explained his motive in possessing himself of Mr. Chartres.

'A doctor!' repeated Caroline.

'Of course, of course,' said Lee, approaching the sofa for the first time. He studied the still unconscious face while Caroline and Briscoe watched him: the first wondering that he should seem to hesitate to send for

a doctor, and the other with an incredulous curiosity.
Briscoe, an ill-natured, half-educated man, had been
seized by a sudden inspiration on seeing the likeness
between Chartres and his brother-in-law. He thought
to overset Lee's new idea by showing him its impractic-
ability. He believed that failure had unhinged his
brother-in-law's mind; and knew for certain that no
argument could possibly avail. He trusted that by
introducing Chartres under such extraordinary circumstances into what he regarded as Lee's insane waking
dream the gross absurdity of it—absurd at least in his
impecunious state—would become apparent to him.
Having once unfixed this idea, he hoped, with the
help of Mrs. Lee, to force his acceptance of the com-
mission for the country weekly. The result was not
going to be what he expected. Lee was taking his
brother's collaboration seriously. A childish smile of
wonder and delight overspread his features, as his likeness to Chartres appeared more fully, in his estimation,
upon a detailed examination. He got a looking-glass,
and compared the two faces, placing the mirror so that
the reflection of his lay as if he had rested his head on
Chartres' shoulder. Thick, soft, grey hair, inclined
still to curl, and divided on the left side; a broad forehead, perpendicular for an inch above the eyebrows,
then sloping inordinately to the beginning of the hair;
eyebrows distinctly marked, but not heavy; a well-
formed nose, rather long, and approaching the aquiline;
full, curved lips; the mouth not small, but liker a

woman's than a man's; the chin, almost feminine, little and rounded; the cheeks smooth, and the face clean shaved. There was no doubt that the men might have been twins, and that their most intimate associates would have been constantly mistaking them.

'It's wonderful — wonderful, Peter!' said Lee. 'What a brilliant stroke of yours this is!'

'But the doctor, Maxwell!' cried Caroline, who was becoming impatient.

'Perhaps we'll not need one,' replied her husband. 'See, he's coming round!'

Chartres began to move uneasily; the blood dawned in his cheeks; and his breathing grew more vigorous. He opened his eyes and attempted to raise his head; but a twinge of pain forced a groan from him, and he again fainted.

'We must get him into bed, in the first place,' said Lee.

With much difficulty this was accomplished. Then Caroline renewed her demand for a doctor; but her husband, professing to have some skill in medicine, declared himself able to treat Chartres, who seemed to have fallen on the top of his head. Cold water, he assured his wife, would soon remove the effects of the concussion. Briscoe also said that there was no need for a doctor. Mrs. Lee did not feel called on to dispute the point; and was about to resume the cold applications, when it struck her, for the first, how very extraordinary a thing it was that this stranger should be in their house.

'Why is he here?' she cried. 'What are you going to do with him?'

'We are going to make use of him in our story, my dear,' said Lee, mildly. 'We will not do him any harm, but we may keep him prisoner here for a little.'

'How cruel! Besides, it would be a crime,' remonstrated his wife.

Lee answered very calmly, but with a consuming fire in his eyes:

'We'll not be cruel if we can possibly help it; and, as for its being criminal, surely no novel is complete without a crime. At the start of this new departure in the art of fiction we will be much hampered in its exercise by scruples and fears of this kind. Some of us may even require to be martyrs. For example: should it be necessary in the course of the story to commit a forgery or a murder, it is not to be expected that the world will allow the crime to pass unpunished. But once the veracity and nobility, the magnanimity and self-sacrifice, which shall characterise this art and the professors of it, have raised the tone of the world, we shall be granted, I doubt not, the most cordial permission to execute atrocities, which, committed selfishly, would brand the criminal as an unnatural monster, but which, performed for art's sake, will redound everlastingly to the credit of the artist.'

Mrs. Lee looked helplessly at her brother, who

whispered to her, 'Leave him to me. I'll make it all right.'

The two men then returned to the parlour, leaving Caroline to wait on Chartres.

Briscoe having cooled down, began to examine the possibilities of good and evil which might spring to himself from his dealing with Chartres. Entered on impulsively as little more than a practical joke; achieved so far with an apparent absolute success—a success which he now felt to be the most remarkable thing about it—this adventure, as he now viewed it, opened up a field for his enterprise which might produce wheat or tares according to his husbandry. He lit a pipe, stretched himself on the sofa, and, closing his eyes, concentrated his thoughts on the remarkable incident which he had brought about.

Lee, whose presence Briscoe had ignored, began to pace the room the moment his brother-in-law's eyes were shut. The stealthy, cat-like glance which he threw at Briscoe expanded to a blaze of triumph as, in one of his turns across the floor, he seized both portmanteaus, and, without accelerating his pace, walked into the unoccupied bedroom, the door of which he locked as softly as he could. Being relieved by Lee's withdrawal, Briscoe gave himself a shake on the sofa, and proceeded with his cogitation.

In the meantime Chartres had revived again. He was unable to use his tongue, but signed by opening his mouth that he wished to eat and drink. He nibbled

a little toast and drank some water.   He then surveyed
the room and his nurse with close attention, and twice
attempted to speak ; but, failing to produce any other
sound than a sigh, he turned his face to the wall and
fell asleep.

Caroline went at once to the parlour, where, of
course, she found her brother alone.

' Peter,' she said, ' what do you wish to do with this
poor man ? '

Briscoe uttered an exclamation of irritation and sat
up to reply.

' What should we do with him ? ' he snarled crustily.
' Nothing, I suppose.   Send him——   Where the
devil are the portmanteaus ? '

' And where's Maxwell ? '

Briscoe was in the lobby immediately.

' Here's his hat ! ' he cried.   ' He's not gone off.'

Before he had time to try the door of the room into
which Lee had shut himself it opened, and that gentleman came forth.   He was scented, gloved, and dressed
in a black broadcloth suit, which had evidently never
been worn before.   He smiled to his brother-in-law,
kissed his wife, and stepped jauntily into the parlour.
They followed, amazed and silent.

' I am Henry Chartres,' he said, drawing a handful
of bank-notes from a bulky purse and offering them to
Caroline.   Briscoe snatched them eagerly, and stowed
them in his breast-pocket.   At that moment the door-
bell rang with a violent peal that paralysed the three.

A visit at any moment was an unusual thing in their household; but Caroline, as she went to open the door, experienced a greater perturbation than she knew how to account for; and her feeling of dread was not lessened when the cabman, who had helped her brother to carry Chartres upstairs, and two policemen entered without ceremony. They walked past her into the parlour.

'Well, constable,' said Lee, addressing the foremost of the two officers, 'what's the matter?'

The constable turned to the cabman, and the cabman looked bewildered. When in the house before he had noticed the striking similarity between Lee and Chartres, and also the great apparent disparity between the social condition of his fare and that of the latter's professed relation. On returning to his stand, he communicated his doubts to the policemen who had been present at the accident. These two sapient Highlanders, after considerable discussion, concluded to call at the house to which the cabman had driven, and, if they found nothing suspicious, excuse their visit in any way suggested. The imaginations of the three had behaved in a felonious manner on the road. Peyton Street had certainly not the cleanest of reputations; and the cabman had got the length of arresting Briscoe's hand in the act of chopping up Chartres' left leg—being the last entire member of his body—when he met the man himself, as he supposed, smiling and as fresh as a daisy.

'We came to see how you were, sir,' said one of the policemen at last.

'Oh, I'm all right now,' said Lee, putting his hand in his pocket. 'I believe you assisted me when I fell. I'll see you downstairs,' with a nod which the constables understood as it was meant. 'I want you,' he said to the cabman, 'to drive me to St. Enoch Station. You'll get my portmanteaus here,' leading him to the bedroom in which he had changed his dress and name.

'Good-bye, Carry. Good-bye, Peter,' and before his wife and brother-in-law had recovered from their surprise, he was rattling away to the station.

CHAPTER II

THE SUITOR AND THE SUED

MISS JANE CHARTRES was a most emphatic talker, because she believed everything she said. Not that she always knew beforehand that what she might be going to say was true; but as soon as she found herself saying anything she believed it firmly from the moment of its announcement. If free-thinking people ever ventured to express a doubt that she might have been misinformed, she gave them her authorities. As the number of witnesses to Miss Jane's word was much too great to admit of their being named separately, she quoted them in the lump, and would silence at once the loudest infidel with a superemphatic, ' Everybody says so,' or ' Everybody does it.'

Miss Jane, being so well acquainted with the sayings and doings of everybody, had been forced to the belief, without knowing French, and with the inconsistency of genius, that everybody was a fool. She did not publish this dogma from the house-tops, but she did most sincerely believe it. About the time that she saw her way clearly to believe in the foolishness of everybody, another faith began to dawn upon her—a faith that she was the only individual in the world who was not a fool. It should hardly be called a faith either; for it never assumed the brightness and consistency of belief, but remained in an uncertain, nebulous condition, perhaps because she never really set herself to examine into the truth of the matter, allowing a sort of flickering halo of infallibility to play about the picture of herself which she beheld in her own mind.

Although she believed that it behoved everybody else, male and female, being fools, to marry, she had come to the conclusion that it behoved her, being in a measure a wise woman, to remain single. This opinion, like all her other opinions—her constant opinions, that is—had been of gradual growth. It was generally supposed that it had fairly taken root about her thirtieth year, when a certain lawyer, who had been a great friend presumably of her brother, discontinued his visits to Snell House, and took to wife the wealthy widow of a game-dealer. It was understood that time had made four prior attempts with the help of a mill-owner, a wealthy farmer, a minister, and a retired colonel, to dibble this opinion with regard to herself and marriage into the soil of Miss Jane's mind. On the marriage of the lawyer with the game-dealer's widow, time made a furious stab with his persevering instrument, and the hardy opinion took a strong hold, and grew, and flourished, and put forth a flower. The opinion was that she ought not to marry; the flower, that she was

made for a higher end than to be the wife of any man.
The fragrance of this flower was grateful to her. However, she never forgot that it was only the blossom of
an opinion, liable to be uprooted, and not the sculptured
ornament of an impossible-to-be-disestablished faith.

At the time when our story begins—the middle of
July, 1880—Miss Jane had been absolute mistress of
Snell House for three months, her brother William, a
bachelor, with whom she had lived for a number of
years, having died suddenly in the spring. A stroke
of apoplexy had overtaken him while walking alone, as
his habit was, on the shore road. His brother, Henry
Chartres, was in India at the time, having gone out
when a young man to push his fortune. Within five
years he had secured by his own energy, and with some
monetary help from his brother, a partnership in a
lucrative business. He then married a lady of some
means, who brought him only one child, a daughter,
called Muriel, after her mother. As is the custom, the
girl was brought to the home-country to be educated,
her father taking a six months' holiday for the purpose
of seeing her safely installed in his brother's house,
where she was to remain for some time, in order to become acclimatised, before going to her first boarding-
school, and also that she might not feel so sorely her
separation from her father and mother, as she would
have done had she gone at once among strangers.
Shortly after the return of Henry Chartres to India his
wife died. He at once determined to give up business

and return to Scotland, where the society of his daughter and relatives would console him for the loss of his wife. But a crisis in the affairs of the Calcutta house of which he was a principal kept him in India. His foresight and resource were absolutely necessary for the weathering of the storm; and he found the relief, which he had been about to seek in Scotland, in an unreserved devotion to business. When he had re-established the credit of his firm more securely than ever, it became apparent that, were he to retire, the consequences might be disastrous for his partners, as his name had come to be synonymous with stability. It was, therefore, not until ten years after the death of his wife that he felt himself at liberty to give up business. The news of his brother's death arrived just as he had begun to arrange his affairs. In reply to a telegram from his sister, he bade her expect him in July; and announced in his first letter that he would manage to reach Scotland about the middle of the month.

The lands of Snell consist of a bit of moor and a park. They had been bought in the beginning of last century by the first notable member of the west country Chartreses, a branch of an old Perthshire family. Miss Jane Chartres refused altogether to admit that she knew anything of the derivation of her ancestor's wealth; and we, therefore, think it needless to refer further to the subject. The wall which bounded Snell Park on the north stood about fifty yards from the edge of a moderately high cliff overlooking the Firth of Clyde. The top of this wall was four feet from the ground within the park, and a little over six feet above the road without. The road was private, and scarcely better than a foot-path.

For three months, then, Miss Jane Chartres, whose character has been indicated above, whose age is left to the reader's charity, had exercised despotic power over Snell House, moor, park, and north wall. But liberties had been taken with that wall, and with an old tree that grew against it. The reader shall hear the history of these dreadful doings from Miss Jane's own lips. She was there, beside the tree, on the afternoon of July 15; and, with her, her friend Mr. Alec Dempster, a very wealthy youth of thirty, with no past—the brother of Emily Dempster, Miss Jane's one bosom friend, whose place in her affections, vacant by death, he supplied in a sort of interim capacity as well as a man with no past, and no possibility of ever having one, could be expected to do.

'Well, Mr. Dempster,' said Miss Jane, 'aren't you dying with wonder to know why I've brought you here?'

'Dying?' said Mr. Dempster, whose voice was a reminiscence of some mechanical sound, one couldn't exactly say which; 'dying is such a strong expression that it almost—eh—ah—expresses the degree of my wonder.'

Mr. Dempster moved his head spirally, slowly and regularly from the top to the bottom of something, as he spoke. That was the great peculiarity of Mr. Dempster: he was like something. Everything about him, from his boots to his manners, bore indefinable resemblances to other things; but the moment a simile seemed securely anchored in some characteristic of his appearance or conduct the characteristic would undulate into something so incongruous with the simile that the latter was like a pair of spectacles on a lynx. One thing only he insisted on reproducing with some degree of regularity of form: the spiral wriggle of his head—extending occasionally into his body—which always accompanied the effort to speak, and sometimes occurred alone.

'Read that,' said Miss Jane, handing Mr. Dempster a letter.

Mr. Dempster, mildly astonished and looking like something very foolish, did as he was directed.

'MY DARLING FRANK,—Meet me to-morrow at five, at the low wall. It's half-past ten, and I am very sleepy. I've been reading history to aunt since eight. I am beginning to dream already, before I am asleep. It's a happy dream—about you! It will become bright and plain when I get to sleep. Good-night, sweetheart.— Your own   MURIEL.'

'What do you think of that?' snapped Miss Jane; and Mr. Dempster looked in all directions hurriedly, as if a whip had been cracked about his ears.

'It's—it's very frank,' he said.

'Very,' went on Miss Jane. 'Look at that.'

She pointed to the bole of the huge elm beneath whose boughs they were standing, indicating a little space denuded of the ivy which covered the rest of the trunk, and extended along the four great arms, and up among the smaller branches of the tree.

Mr. Dempster bored his nose into the uncovered bark, studied it from several points of view, bending and curvetting and bridling with as much ado as if he had been an antiquary in presence of a newly-discovered inscription.

' "M C, F H," ' he said at length ; 'inside a heart— very pretty and—ah—suggestive ; but—commonplace.'

Mr. Dempster's pauses, however arbitrary, were impressive.

'Do you know whose these initials are ?' Miss Jane asked.

'I haven't the remotest idea.'

' "M C," Muriel Chartres ; "F H," Frank Hay.'

'Ah !'

Dempster leant against an arm of the tree and regarded Miss Jane blankly. He had arrived from Edinburgh that day at her summons, to meet Mr. Chartres, who was expected in the afternoon, and to prosecute his suit for the hand of Muriel. This was a dash of cold water right in his face. He hadn't a word to say, and scarcely any breath to say one.

'You know Mr. Hay,' Miss Jane said. 'You remember, William used to patronise him.'

'The foundling! Why, the fellow hasn't a penny!' exclaimed Dempster.

'Ah, Mr. Dempster,' said Miss Jane more sweetly than her wont, 'presumption is poverty's next door neighbour, wealth and modesty often go hand in hand.'

Dempster at once applied this aphoristic compliment to himself, as he was intended to do; but he horrified Miss Jane by bowing emphatically in acknowledgment, and he outraged her further by endeavouring to pay her back in kind :

'A thorough acquaintance with the world generally accompanies the single life.'

That was his period, and he imagined he had acquitted himself fairly well. But dissatisfaction lowered in Miss Jane's brow. He proceeded with stammering haste to mend matters :

'Especially the single female—eh—ah——'

An angry flush drew him up. Still, he went at it again headlong, smiling too, and in as suave a tone as he could command :

'Wisdom is an old maid—I mean—Minerva was unmarried.'

Everybody knows people like Mr. Dempster. We are accustomed to their shifting similitudes, their inability to express themselves, their pretensions, and their good nature. In fact, we do not regard them—we do not recognise that they are peculiar; and when we see one of them singled out and reproduced—on the stage, for example—however faithfully, we call it caricature. Miss Jane had a very narrow circle of acquaintances. The Chartreses, indeed, were all proud originals. For several generations they had mingled little in society, preferring to retain their angularities of character in all the ruggedness of nature, rather than submit to the painful process of grinding on the social wheel, by which jagged, dull-veined flints are smoothed and polished. Miss Jane could not tolerate ordinary people. Dempster was the only commonplace character in whom she had any interest. His visits to Snell House had been hitherto few and short, and she had never got accustomed to his genial stupidity. Ineptitude with Miss Jane was an almost unpardonable offence. She remembered, however, in the confusion to which he had reduced her, much necessity in the past for self-denial and longsuffering on his account, and, having a real regard for him, she calmed her troubled soul, saying to herself, 'He means well.' And then aloud:

'Now, Mr. Dempster, this is the low wall Muriel speaks of. This letter I found here.'

She pushed aside some large ivy leaves in one of the forks of the elm, and deposited the letter in a deep, natural crevice—the bottom of which was quite invisible, although easily reached by the hand.

'How did you know to search there?' Asked Dempster.

'Because I knew Muriel was in love.'

'Did she tell you?'

'No, no; this was the way of it.'

Miss Jane was in her element. She leant against the bole of the tree and folded her arms across her belt.

'I observed that she had acquired a habit of going about with her eyebrows absurdly elevated, with a languishing look in her eyes, and with her lips just touching each other; but evidently ready at a moment's notice to open and sigh, or to compress and kiss. I know very well what these signs meant in a girl of her age. Just raise your eyebrows, Mr. Dempster.'

Mr. Dempster raised his eyebrows.

'No, no! not to the extent of expressing astonishment, but in this way. See.'

Miss Jane suited the action to the word.

'When you raise your eyebrows that way your eyes can't help a languishing expression. Then this is the way her mouth was.'

Miss Jane made a *moue*.

'If you don't care to do it before me, do it when you are alone, and you will find that raising your eyebrows and looking at nothing, and preparing the lips to open, will produce in you a relaxed, sentimental, self-pitying kind of feeling, which is pretty like what romantic girls feel when they are in love. Of course, in Muriel's case it was the feeling which produced the expression, and not the expression the feeling; but I know very well that an assumption of the expression can produce the

feeling, and that it always conveys the idea of that feeling to those who see it. It's the same with all feelings.'

The whole man Dempster had listened to this exposition, and burst out earnestly, 'Miss Chartres, your
experience amazes me! Your observation is that of a
keen—eh—ah—observer; and your discernment is truly
marvellous !'

He always tried to talk in newspaper paragraphs,
but his efforts were seldom attended with the success
they merited.

Miss Jane shrugged her shoulders and continued :
'My suspicions were confirmed yesterday. I followed
her here and secured this letter. I thought it right
that you, as a suitor for Muriel's hand, favoured by me,
and doubtless to be favoured by her father, should be
informed of the matter.'

'You overpower me with kindness,' blurted Dempster. 'And you'll stand by me, Miss Chartres ? You'll
be my go-between—I mean my bulwark, my bottle-
holder ?' He was full of imagery, but he qualified it,
saying plaintively : ' I can't express myself lucidly
and vividly, like you ; but everybody knows I mean
well.'

'I think we understand each other, Mr. Dempster,'
said Miss Jane, looking at her watch. ' A quarter to
five. We'd better go. Muriel will be here immediately.
Of course I haven't told her that I have discovered this
clandestine correspondence. I shall put the matter into

her father's hands this very day, and leave him to deal with her.'

Dempster assented to this as a wise proceeding. 'It would hardly do to watch the meeting here, I suppose— that is, if there is a meeting,' he said, as they left the wall.

'To play the spy, Mr. Dempster! No, not that.'

The ivy-clad elm in which Miss Jane had found Muriel's letter, and in which she now left it forgetfully, was believed by the school-boys to mark the burial-place of a Roman general. It certainly looked as if it might be fourteen hundred years old, or even as old as the Christian era. It was a worthy peer of the Mongewell, Chipstead, and Spratborough elms, by the hoary roughness of its bark, where that could be seen, by its portly waist, and wide-spread arms, drooping gracefully to the ground, by its magnificent cone of foliage, and its fathomless depth of green. How pleasant Muriel found it to stand under, to lean against, to delight her eyes with its shapeliness, and bathe her sight in its ocean of colour! And then, with all its old-world dignity, how tender it was! How safe in its arms she felt! She could think and dream there like Nature herself, conscious and glad that the elm knew all about it. When she forced her way among the drooping boughs up to the mighty bole, she was sure that the tree thrilled with happiness, and she heard it murmuring— murmuring under its spicy breath. No wonder she made it her trysting-tree!

As soon as Miss Jane and Dempster returned to the house, Muriel, who had been lying on the lawn pretending to read a newspaper, arose, and, still apparently engrossed by the news, took a circuitous route to the elm. When she got beyond the range of prying eyes, the deceptive newspaper was folded, and, carrying it in one hand behind her, and in the other swinging by the strings her garden-hat, she sped along, fearful lest Frank should have to wait. Half over the wall she stretched herself, and looked up and down the road. She was first. She leant against the tree and gazed before her. She felt perfectly happy. He was sure to come ; and that was the horizon—the end of the world. There was nothing beyond the little quarter of an hour that was dawning like a new era. She would hardly be so happy when he, the sun of it, came to kiss her.

Now she looked out through the screen of leaves, softening the light upon their scabrous cheeks, and showering it like dew from their downy breasts, and saw, latticed by the wiry, corky branches and bright brown callow twigs, the violet Firth, smooth, velvety, the pasture of white gulls, whose cries come faintly up ; glimpses of the opposite shore, with the sparkling houses of the summer towns ; the lordly sweep of the entrance to Loch Long ; the purple misty crowns of the Cobbler and Ben Donich ; and the sky ; and a shadow——

‘ Frank ! ’

'How glad I am to find you here!' he said. 'I was foolish enough to fear you mightn't come.'

'Why did you doubt? I never missed meeting you yet.'

'Then you expected me! I was sure at the bottom of my heart that you would be here.'

'Did I expect you! What are you thinking of? There's something the matter. How could you possibly be afraid that I mightn't come after I had asked you to meet me?'

'But you didn't ask me.'

'Oh! Did you not get my message?'

'No; and I visited our letter-box last night and this morning.'

She tore her arm from his, and plunged her hand into the fork of the tree. A shock passed through her as she felt her letter. She knew in a moment it had been violated. The thought that another than he for whom it was intended had read it thrilled her with an exquisite pang. Her whole face and neck flushed crimson. She drew out the paper, crushed it small, and thrust it into her pocket.

'The mean, shameful spy!' she hissed.

Youth has no mercy in a case of this kind.

'See,' she continued, panting, 'I put it here this morning at eight. It was gone at ten. Now it is here again. The traitor!'

'Is it a man?' asked Frank.

'No! It's——'

She had grown pale, and she blushed again. She looked at him with flickering eyelids. The foolish fellow's pride in Muriel at that moment made him heart-sick; the lump was in his throat, and, had he been un-observed, the moisture which stood in his eyes would have overflowed. Even in the first wild anger at betrayal she would not betray again. He placed his arm about her and she sobbed; one sob, and then one tear out of each eye; and with that she mastered her-self.

'Frank,' she said, as if the discovery had not been made, 'you know my father will be here to-day. He may have come while I've been talking to you. Will you speak to him to-night? I don't want to have a secret from him. Will you? You needn't be fright-ened. I haven't seen him since I was nine; but I know that he's like you, gentle and manly--just a gentle-man. Make up your mind now—quick, quick, quick! And let me away, or I'll be late for dinner.'

And so it was arranged that they should see each other at the low-walk again at eight that evening, lest there should be any reason why Frank might not speak at once to Mr. Chartres.

CHAPTER III

ON THE ROAD

LEE secured a compartment for himself in the Greenock train. He had a large bundle of letters, taken from one of Chartres' portmanteaus, with him. These he studied with an intensity which he had never bestowed on anything before. He selected some dozen for perusal, and was still devouring them when the train arrived at Princes Pier.

As he stepped on the platform he reeled and was only saved from falling by the porter who opened the door of the compartment in which he had travelled. This weakness was the result of the strain of the last two hours. He fortified himself with a glass of brandy and a sandwich, deposited the portmanteaus in the left-luggage office; and started to walk to Gourock.

He was a tall man, with more than proportionate length of limb. Walking had always been his favourite exercise, and he looked along the Greenock esplanade from the summit of the approach to the station with a shining eye. All the world has admired it from the deck of the *Columba*; but to walk along it at a good spanking pace, feeling its costly breadth, its substantiality, its triumph over nature ; to be conscious of the solid nineteenth-century comfort and luxury that line one side of it, ascending the hill to larger villas and more spacious grounds ; and to be, as Lee became, before he was two minutes on the road, part and parcel of the sky-blue lake-like firth, whose water murmured, for the tide was full, with soft reproach against the curbing bastion ; of the shining magical houses on the other side ; of the green and golden shoreward slopes ; of the depths and heights of the purple mountains that met the sky—to be drunk with the sunlight and the sea, with the merging, glowing, fading wealth of colour, and the far-reaching romance of the hills, is to enjoy to the full this west-country esplanade.

When he arrived at the end of it, Lee, unable to endure the ordinary road, jumped on a car and took a seat on the top.

He was now in a mood to dare anything, and continued his revel in the splendid July afternoon, for the brain-sick man was a poet.

Through Gourock and Ashton the car rattled, but, wrapped in his own dream, he saw nothing of them.

From the terminus he walked confidently along the shore road. He felt that he would know Snell House the moment he beheld it. Then there would be no difficulty. Chartres could not be expected to remember any of the domestics ; besides, in ten years it was more than likely that they had all been changed twice over. His sister and daughter—he could not possibly mistake them. He would be shy a little, undemonstrative, uncommunicative, and plead his long journey—for Chartres had travelled from London on the preceding night—as an excuse for retiring early. Then——

A sudden slap on the shoulder interrupted his reverie, and, wheeling round, he confronted Briscoe, on whose face a bitter sneer was varnished over with a grin at the surprise and annoyance his appearance caused his brother-in-law.

'This way,' said Briscoe; and Lee followed him in silence.

They found a seat, one of a number placed along the shore between the Cloch and Ashton. There was a considerable slope from the road to the water's edge; and they were securely concealed from the eyes of pedestrians by the trees and bushes that line stretches of the sea-board.

It never entered Lee's head to ask Briscoe how he came to be there. Had he done so, Briscoe would have told him—that is, if he had thought the truth expedient—how Caroline and he, after Lee's sudden and daring departure from Peyton Street, judged it the best course to intercept him at the St. Enoch station; but how he, Briscoe, having already in his breast-pocket some of the advantages arising from Lee's deception, determined, if possible, to add to them, and so journeyed to Greenock in the same train with his brother-in-law;

and, pushing on before him, waited for him at a quiet part of the road, where they might discuss the situation without much fear of interruption or observation. He had not the remotest intention of aiding Lee, whom he despised, to pursue his deception to a successful issue. On the contrary, he intended to line his own pockets as thickly as he could, and get off to London that night or the following morning. There was one risk: Chartres might recover sufficiently to come down to Snell House before he had gone. This risk he determined to run.

'I wish,' said Lee, recovering speedily from his surprise, 'you had not come down yet. I have been thinking of you and Caroline, and don't exactly see what to do with you.'

His infatuation was such that he had no doubt Briscoe intended to collaborate with him.

'I might marry you,' he continued, 'to my daughter Muriel; or, as she is perhaps too young, to my mature sister, Jane. But what to do with Caroline? You see, I didn't marry again in India. The only course I can conceive at present, will be to make her acquaintance as it were for the first time, and marry her over again. But there's no hurry; and, I think, on the whole, you had better return to Glasgow until I prepare matters for you down here.'

'Mr. Chartres,' said Briscoe, 'am I to collaborate with you, or am I not?'

Lee flushed with pleasure, and answered, 'Most certainly, my dear Peter!'

'Then I must have some share in devising the plot.'

'Assuredly! I beg your pardon. I was forgetting your rights. Really, I have been selfish in the solitary enjoyment of the creation of this novel, which you began with such originality and power.'

Briscoe rather winced at this. However, he was glad to find Lee so tractable.

'Mr. Chartres,' he said, 'I am your friend, Mr. Peter Briscoe. I came from India with you. I'm a rough diamond; don't care how I dress—accounts for my rather worn toggery; see? Saved you from drowning when you fell overboard in the Bay of Biscay. You, eternally grateful; I, no friends in this country—across for a visit merely—came right north with you, agreeing to do so at the last moment, so that you had no time to advise them at Snell House.'

Lee gazed at his brother-in-law with admiration.

'Briscoe, my dear fellow,' he cried, 'you're a trump! You—you saved my life.'

'Then we'll take the road again,' said Briscoe. 'The house is round the corner; I inquired shortly before you came up.'

'Briscoe,' said Lee, 'for the first work of a newly-born art, we are——'

'Beating the record.'

'Exactly, my rough and ready friend.'

CHAPTER IV

A HEAVY FATHER

'Now, Jane, let me understand this about Muriel. You say she is at present engaged in a grand love affair with some young hopeful or other.'

'Yes, Henry. Frank Hay is a very good-looking, clever, well-behaved young man. He has taken one of the big bursaries in Glasgow University, and looks forward to a professorship somewhere. These prospects are rather mediocre, especially in connection with a Chartres; but neither William nor I would have said a word against him were he not a foundling.'

'A foundling! How very interesting! An actual foundling.'

'O, there's nothing unusual about his case. I forget the exact details, but they differ in no essential from what we are accustomed to in stories.'

'That's rather unfortunate. I should have liked everything connected with these events to have the same characteristic as the main circumstance, distinct novelty.'

'What do you mean, Henry? Muriel is right in thinking you curiously changed.'

'Does she think so? Well; I should have stuck by my original determination, and gone to bed; but I felt so invigorated after dinner, that I thought we might as well have a talk over matters this evening.'

'Yes,' said Miss Jane, dryly, prodding Lee all over with her piercing eyes.

'Do you think,' she queried, 'we did right in forbidding Muriel to have any communication with Mr. Hay?'

'Well, my dear sister, you must see that the question of right hardly enters here. It is purely a matter of adapting means to an end. Should the course you have followed, as in the case of a pair of high-spirited lovers, be calculated to lead to strained relations, and produce, say, an elopement, I should be inclined to support you; as, although shorn of much of its romance in these days of railways and telegraphs, there is always a measure of excitement to be got out of a runaway match.'

Miss Jane meditated for several seconds; and hopefully came to the conclusion that her brother had developed a satirical tendency, which he gratified in this recondite fashion. She made no reply. Lee resumed.

'I think you had better send Muriel to me. I would like to have a talk with her alone.'

'Very well,' said Miss Jane curtly, and left the room.

It was the library in which Lee sat. He had

arrived with Briscoe about six o'clock, just as the Snell household were sitting down to dinner. Four was the usual dinner hour, but it had been put off till five and then till six—to the anger and horror of the cook—in the hope that Mr. Chartres would be there to preside. Both Lee and Briscoe imagined that the dinner had gone off to admiration. The latter, taking advantage of his rollicking character, was now roving about the rooms, helping himself to many little valuables. After securing all the money Lee was possessed of, which he might manage to do that evening, he saw a fair chance of getting away with his booty, out of immediate danger, and before the arrival of Chartres, whom he half-expected to find in every room he entered. He knew that Caroline would not wait for his return if her charge recovered sufficiently to travel, but would start with him at once; and while she might be able to make terms for her crazy husband, some stout men-servants and a duck-pond suggested anything but a pleasant ending to his own share in the adventure. After Miss Jane had left the library, Lee, with a most placid expression, walked across the room once or twice, and sat down to wait for Muriel. In a second or two the door opened, and Mr. Dempster appeared. This gentleman had been left to himself since dinner, and was searching for Miss Jane.

'I beg your pardon, sir,' he said, looking the very picture of a square man in a round hole. 'I thought Miss Chartres was here.'

'Come in, come in, Mr. Dempster,' said Lee, blandly. 'Is it my daughter or my sister you wish to see?'

'Your sister, sir.'

'I expect them both here in a few minutes. Take a seat.'

Dempster gathered his coat-tails on either side with as much tenderness and delicacy as if they had been growing out of him and were recovering from rheumatism, and sat down on the very edge of a chair, crowding himself together as if he had consisted of several people.

'I hope I don't intrude,' said Dempster, with the spiral motion of his head. He was always more uncomfortable and serpentine than usual in the presence of strangers.

'Not at all.'

Lee said to himself, 'This is a millionaire; and I am an adventurer—Fortune is a mistress of irony.'

A smile peculiar to him, and childish in its unconcealed expression of pleasure, passed over his face. Then he said brusquely, but with perfect good humour, 'Do you think much, Mr. Dempster?'

'Think!' exclaimed Mr. Dempster, throwing his head back in a convolution which a burlesque actor would have paid highly to learn the trick of.

'Yes, think,' repeated Lee, with his happy, innocent smile.

'I—I can't say I do,' said Dempster, perspiring profusely. 'I—I,' he continued making a wholly ineffectual effort to laugh—'I—eh—ah—haven't given the subject much attention. But——'

'Exactly, Mr. Dempster, I understand. I have often thought by the way, that you unlucky fellows who inherit your money, can't enjoy it so well as we who have wrought for it.'

Now, if there was one thing Dempster objected to more than another, it was to be hurried about from subject to subject. He had just got his mind focussed to the consideration of Lee's first question, when a new distance intervened, and—he saw men as trees walking. But he must make some reply.

'No—no,' he said. 'We can't. I—I think we can't. Eh—ah——'

'Eh—ah,' the favourite expletive of the orator, was frequently employed by Dempster with a solemn pathos inexpressibly touching. Lee almost relented at the overpowering sadness of its utterance on this occasion; but the baiting of a millionaire was as novel as any of his present manifold pleasures, and he continued it.

'I suppose now,' he said, 'you would like to work hard at something or other. Most idle men would.'

Dempster rubbed his knees with vehemence, anxious, doubtless, to get himself into an electric condition which would enable him to overcome the insane disposition he felt to fall forward at Lee's feet. He succeeded in producing so much of the positive fluid as to fall back instead of forward; but all he could manage to say was, 'I suppose I would.'

'I have often wondered,' said Lee, whose smile was beginning to be warped by malice, 'why rich men don't commit burglaries and homicides in order to obtain terms of hard labour. It would be such an absolute change for them; *ennui* would hide its head.'

It is impossible to say what ultimate effect this remarkable suggestion would have had upon Dempster, for the paralysis which it caused to begin with was suddenly cured by a tap—a shrinking, single tap on the door, preceding the entrance of Muriel. Dempster took the opportunity of escaping in a thoroughly graceless manner. When the door had closed again, Lee said to Muriel, who remained standing, 'Do you not find me exactly what you expected?'

She looked hard at him. It was on her lips to tell him that she thought him very unlike his letters; but she merely said, 'You are not like your photographs.'

'No; they were generally thought good in India.'

'O, anyone could tell for whom they were meant.'

'Of course. My appearance has changed since I last sat to a photographer. Sit down, Muriel; I wish to have some serious conversation with you.'

Muriel sat down on a couch. Her eyes were twinkling, and the blood danced into her cheeks.

'I have learned from your aunt,' said Lee, who was just a little too portentously grave, 'that there exists a romantic attachment between a certain Mr. Frank Hay and you. I understand you are firmly persuaded that you and this gentleman love each other with an unchangeable love. I will grant that Mr. Hay is a handsome, high-spirited young man. I do not remember to have seen him; but I give my daughter credit for not falling in love with a booby. I admit that first love is the most ecstatically delightful thing in the world. I say, I subscribe to all that and as much more as you like in the same strain; but—' and here he became very severe—'I have to inform you that from this day you must cease to see, or correspond with Mr. Frank Hay.'

'O father!'

Lee, enjoying his power, and as much a spectator of the scene as an actor in it, continued coldly, ' It will be hard I know; but your friends have acted very wisely in coming between you. Girls should never be allowed to choose husbands, and never are in well-regulated families. You may think me plain-spoken and harsh, perhaps; but I have a habit of coming to the point; and, notice, of never returning to it. The matter is settled.'

' But, sir——'

' What! have I not said it is settled? I do not mean, however, to do you out of a husband.'

Muriel shivered, and her face became white.

' My friend, Mr. Briscoe, who saved my life is still a young man; and I intend to have him for a son-in-law.'

Lee's eyes dilated with exultation. His novel was going to turn out a masterpiece.

'Marry Mr. Briscoe!'

'It rests with him,' said Lee.

'What! Your daughter must marry this Mr. Briscoe if he wants her, whether she likes or not?'

'I am glad,' said Lee in a truly regal style, 'that you apprehend the matter so clearly.'

'I am bewildered,' said Muriel.

'You seem to be; but it is wise of you not to object. I hope to find you always a dutiful daughter.'

Lee left the room. A time-piece on the mantel-shelf rang eight. The blood returned to Muriel's cheeks, and she ran out of the house to the north wall.

CHAPTER V

THE ART OF PROPOSING

WHEN Dempster left the library on the entrance of Muriel, he met Miss Jane at the door of that room. She proposed a turn in the park as the evening was doing honour to the glorious day. They went out together and wandered to Muriel's elm. Dempster's suit was the subject they discussed. She urged him to make a proposal that night, and promised to procure him an opportunity. Dempster was willing, but in great straits how to proceed.

'You see,' he said, 'I never did a thing of the kind before. Then you know Muriel is not aware that I'm in love with her. If she knew that, then I could go at it like a—professor.'

It is to be feared he intended to say 'nigger,' and only substituted the more refined but equally enigmatic word by an exhaustive effort of brain power, whose external manifestation was the usual wriggle.

Miss Jane said, 'Well it *is* very difficult to know what to do in making an offer of marriage. I have had six proposals—that is, formal proposals—all of which I refused peremptorily, as I think that I was made for a higher end than to be the wife of any man—and they were all done differently; but, on the whole, I prefer the colonel's method; and I think in proposing to Muriel you had better follow it.'

'Oh, thank you! Tell me exactly what he did, and I'll practise it just now.'

In his excitement Dempster's body, lithe and lissom as that of the most poetical maiden, partook in the motion of his head. Miss Jane, who had often been on the point of speaking to him about this absurd habit, burst out, 'Don't wriggle that way, as if you were impaled!'

Dempster shrivelled up, and hung flaccid on his spinal column, like a hooked worm that has been long in the water.

'I assure you,' continued Miss Jane, less harshly, 'if you are ever to take a place in the world you must overcome that.'

'Must I! I'm very glad you've told me. It's my natural form.'

'Conquer it, conquer it. Remember Demosthenes, Mr. Dempster.'

'I will, I will,' he cried, almost breaking his back, and causing a hot shooting pain in his head, as he nipped a sprouting corkscrew in the bud—a metaphor worthy of himself. Then he made a sudden plunge into a sea of words, where he had to keep perpetually rapping on the head an electric eel that tried with unremitting fervour to run, or rather wriggle, the gauntlet of his body and escape by his skull through the suture.

'Miss Chartres' he said, 'I wish you would help me. I have been wanting to get married for six years now, and I can't. I won't be caught. They try it, the mothers. They dangle their daughters before me like —like Mayflies. But I won't bite. I'd sooner starve, Miss Chartres, starve. Die in a ditch—celibacy, you know. I'll never marry one of these artificial flies. They may be good enough; but it's their mothers—O, their mothers! Why, I've read about them in novels. And then, when I do fall in love with a nice—with a sweet—a natural—eh—ah—a natural fly—you understand—I—I can't bite—haven't the courage—don't know how. I've been in love before several times— though I never loved anybody before like Muriel—and I couldn't possibly manage to—to bite. But you'll teach me now, my dear Miss Chartres.'

He emerged, dripping, and the long-repressed eel shot out at the crown of his head in a rapid spasm, leaving him a mere husk propped against the elm.

Miss Jane, who had made up her mind that he should marry Muriel, put his sincerity against his *gaucherie*, and determined to drill him into some better form; for she judged that if the excitement of talking about a proposal produced effects of the kind she had witnessed, that of making one would simply stultify its object.

'I'll help you,' she said. 'Stand there.'

She seated herself on a protruding root of the elm,

and pointed to a sort of alcove in one of the large
boughs. Dempster squeezed himself under the
branches, and stood, or rather stooped, at attention.

'Now, obey my instructions. Imagine this to be a
drawing-room. Come forward on tip-toe, and say very
significantly, and in fact intensely, " Good evening, Miss
Chartres," and don't wriggle.'

Dempster, clothed with resolution as with a strait-
jacket, advanced, and whispered between his set teeth,
' Good evening, Miss Chartres.'

' Good evening, Mr. Dempster; be seated.'

He looked about for as comfortable a knot as
possible, but Miss Jane cried, ' No, no! you must
refuse respectfully. The gallant colonel did. He said
something like this :—" Miss Chartres, I will never sit in
your presence until I have got an answer to a question
which my whole being is burning to ask." When you
have said that, go down on one knee and take my hand.'

Dempster was beginning to feel at home, Miss
Jane was so sympathetic, and smiled so benignly. In
the heat of the moment, and to prove himself an apt
scholar, he thought he would reproduce his lesson with
variations. So he got down on his knees at the off-set,
and began, ' My adored Miss Chartres, never again in
your enchanting presence——'

' O! ' went off among the branches like a sharp tap
on a muffled drum.

Miss Jane looked up in time to catch a glimpse of
Muriel's head. Dempster's strait-jacket snapped, and

the released mechanism hoisted him to his feet, spinning and glaring round in a vortex of coat-tails.

Miss Jane, also on her feet, said calmly, 'That was Muriel. There's no harm done. I must just tell her the exact state of the case. It's always best to tell the truth. If she has any heart at all it will be touched at the thought of your rehearsing your proposal. I'll go after her, and explain, and send her to you. That's the very thing.'

Now Miss Jane was a very shrewd woman. Her mind had been ingenuously fixed on a marriage between her niece and her *protégé* up to the moment of the appearance of Muriel's head among the branches. There and then a sense of the incongruity of such a union had struck her with most convincing power. Several forces converged in this blow. One can be mentioned unreservedly, viz., the sudden intuitive recognition of the fact that Muriel would never consent to marry Dempster. Another, equally powerful, must only be hinted :— the lady at that moment had once more, however strangely, a gentleman at her feet. These are the keys to her future conduct.

She was about to go after Muriel, but Dempster clutched her dress.

'I can't,' he whimpered.

'Nonsense. You'll be astonished at your own courage.'

'But the proposal. How am I to say it?'

'Keep a good heart, and remember my instructions.

I've told you how to begin. The rest you must do for yourself. Muriel will be here shortly.'

Dempster resigned himself: and in a few seconds fear wound him up to a pitch of nervous excitement, abnormal even with him.

'I'll rehearse again,' he said aloud, withdrawing to the alcove. He got into the strait-jacket once more, and advanced on tip-toe to an imaginary lady. But the charge did not give him satisfaction. He retreated and stepped out a second time. He was too absorbed in his manœuvres to remember that however perfect he might become, this mode would be out of the question in the impending interview.

'Good evening,' he said impressively to the mossy root, and got down on his knees.

'Miss Chartres'—and persuasion tipped his tongue —'I am burning to know——'

A silvery ripple glided through the air behind him. 'I beg' pardon, Mr. Dempster. I was not aware you were so pious a man,' said Muriel.

A jack-in-the-box when the spring is touched shoots up not more suddenly than Dempster did. Abashed, he could only stammer, 'Eh-ah—I mean well.'

'I do indeed believe you,' said Muriel in a kindly tone. 'My aunt has told me that you were about to honour me with an offer of marriage. I thank you, sir; but I beg you not to put me to the necessity—the very disagreeable necessity—of refusing you.'

Half-an-hour before she could not have taken such a plain-spoken initiative; but the interview with Lee had roused her soul to arms.

Dempster, on the contrary, dimly conscious of his own absurdity and afraid to trust his nature, stood forth against her in his strait-waistcoat of formality. He could hardly believe his ears, accustomed to the lie that no girl could possibly refuse a millionaire, a false tenet which he had donned with his first pair of trousers.

'Why should you refuse me? I—I am very rich, and I love you.' This was still pronounced in his best society tone.

'I am very sorry for you,' said Muriel frigidly. 'If you persist you will only annoy us both.'

His fear suddenly left him. He felt an underhand attack upon his wealth, which was *him*—his personality. He threw off the strait-waistcoat. He turned up the sleeves of his riches, and, in a raucous tone like that of an aggrieved school bully who wants an excuse to pommel a small boy, said 'Why do you refuse me? Give me a reason.'

'A reason!'

'Yes. Is there anything extraordinary in asking for a reason? I can't be put off in this way, you know. Do you love another?'

'I am very sorry for you; but you are becoming impertinent.'

'But what am I to do if you won't marry me? All my friends know what I've come here for. It's absurd.'

'You had better desist.'

It is charitable to suppose that Dempster was utterly unaware of what he was doing. Anger nearly suffocated him. He twisted and squirmed at every word, writhing with the anticipation of mockery.

'It's shameful,' he cried. 'Here have I been loving you like—like lava ; and to be thrown overboard, ignominiously—yes, ignominiously'—he fancied he heard the word resounding in smoking-rooms—'for a poor nobody.'

Muriel started and glared at him. But he was 'fey,' and went on.

'You may well look ! A foundling—a charity-boy ! You love this sup—superfluous and probably illegitimate pauper, who——'

'O, you unmanly fool !'

'I say !' and he fell against the tree smitten by Muriel's thunder and lightning. The storm pealed on.

'I have read of men who spoke such cowardice, but I never thought to know one. How dare you talk of love ? O the shame ! Every wealthy fool can look at us, and love us, as they say, and whine to us—it *is* a shame ! What right have you to love me or think of me ? If you ever wish to be worth a thought, or fit for his service whom you've slandered, go and found hospitals, endow scholarships—fling your wealth in the sea—only get rid of it ! And plough the fields, break stones, dig ditches—some honest work your scanty brains are suited for ; and when that has made you something of a man, go and beg his pardon. Go away from here, now, at once. He's waiting for me.'

Dempster limped away. His works were all run down. Youth is cruel, and Muriel had meant to wound; but she felt a little remorseful at the sight of the abject creature she had scorched and scotched with such crude severity, and wished that she had at least spared him the last savage cut. To be called a fool and a coward— to be told to get rid of one's personality, is bad ; but to be dismissed in order to make instant room for the other, partakes too much of hacking and slashing, and might even be put in the category with vitriol-throwing.

Muriel looked over the wall and called Frank. He was waiting somewhere near, she knew ; and he came and climbed over and kissed her.

'Where were you hiding ?' she asked.

'I sat on a stone by the side of the wall, and meant to sit there till the voices ceased, or you called me.'

'Did you hear what we said ?'

'No.'

'Well, it doesn't matter just now. I'll tell you some other time.'

She sat down on the wall and bade him do the same. Dempster was forgotten : the stronger impression, that produced by Lee, came out through the more recent one like the original writing on a palimpsest.

'When one meets one's father,' she said, 'after a long absence, whether one knows him well or not, one's heart leaps, and a great thrill strikes through one.'

'Yes,' said Frank. 'I believe my nerves would ring to the sound of my father's voice if I were hearing it, though I've never seen him.'

'Don't imagine it for a moment, dear. When your father comes back after ten years you shiver in his presence—you feel as if you had jumped into a frosty sea out of the summer. I did when I went to him from you.'

She kicked her heels against the wall, and sat on her hands, looking round and up at Frank like a bird. Then she turned her gaze into the tree. In the mood that held her, to think was to resolve. She came to her feet, and stood before her lover.

'What would you think if I were to tell you that my father had chosen a husband for me?'

'I should think it the height of folly, unless I were his selection.'

'Come to him now. Say to him that you love me, and that I love you, and that he may kill me if he likes, but that I will never marry anybody else.'

'This is encouraging.'

'And you will need courage.'

'What is wrong?'

'You'll know soon enough. Come.' And she led him to the house. She danced along the path. Her eyes clashed against his.

'I'm in the major key,' she said.

No wonder she was in the major key. She had a vision of the encounter between her lover and her father ; a wordy tournament in which the former bore off the honours. Her heart was fast melting down every feeling into a glowing rage at the man who, after ten years' absence, came to blight her life ; and her body, the flames about that crucible, leapt and trembled. She could move only in bounds to a measure. Frank, mystified, but flushed by sympathy, followed her, admiring.

She took him straight to the library. Lee was not there.

'Wait here, and I shall find my father,' she said.

But Miss Jane came into the room.

'How in the name of all the proprieties dare you enter this house, sir ? ' she cried.

Frank, as the reader will surmise, had been forbidden the house.

Muriel sat down on the couch and pulled her lover to her side. Then she rested her elbows on her knees and her chin in her hands, and looked at her aunt. It was grossly impertinent.

'For shame! What is the meaning of this folly, Muriel ? ' and the angry lady crossed the floor, and bristled before the couple with only a yard between.

Muriel became absolutely but serenely rabid.

'Mr. Hay is going to take supper with us to-night,' she said. 'Ring the bell please, aunt, and order supper to be hastened.'

Miss Jane towered, physically and morally.

'Muriel '—she spoke solemnly, as became her exaltation—'you wicked girl!   You have much greater cause to keep your room and cry over your misdemeanours, than come here outraging all decency in this way.   Have you no maidenly reserve at all?'

Then she leant towards Frank.

'Mr. Hay, I should think this exhibition of temper and impudence will make it needless to fear that you will aid further in thwarting our intentions with regard to Muriel.   Indeed, I don't know at present how it will be possible for me to stand by quietly and see any young man, however eligible, throw himself away on such an incorrigible young woman.'

Thoroughly on fire at the imperturbable smile on Muriel's face, she leaned towards her again, a flaming tower of Pisa.

'Muriel, if ever you wish to regain the place you have lost in my esteem, you will tell Mr. Hay to leave this house at once, and never enter it again.'

Muriel fumbled in her pocket, and half-withdrew her hand, but thought better of it.

Miss Jane again menaced Frank.

'Mr. Hay, the cool effrontery you display in sitting quietly smiling—don't try to hide it, sir!—while the woman you profess to love throws to the winds all respect for herself and her betters, actually and openly defying her aunt——'

Muriel had risen, and was approaching the bell-pull. Her hand was almost on it, when her aunt, with surprising agility, intercepted her.

' Not while I live ! ' she cried, almost hysterically.

Frank rose, and began, ' I shall not——'

' You shall ! ' cried Muriel.

' Leave the room, Muriel ! ' said Miss Jane, collecting her dignity, and posing again as a tower.

Muriel's hand slipped back to her pocket, and she looked straight into her aunt's eyes. Once more she changed her purpose, and left the room with a smile, and an airy nod to Frank.

' Did that girl wink just now, sir ? ' said Miss Jane.

' I didn't observe.'

The excited lady pulled a chair before Frank, and sat down opposite him.

' Mr. Hay,' she said, ' I wish to be reasonable. I know myself what it is to be young. Indeed, putting other circumstances aside, I can almost sympathise with you in your infatuation for Muriel. She is really a very good-looking girl; but this scene must have convinced you that her nature is wholly unregenerate, and I hope——'

What she hoped can only be guessed, for Muriel re-entered the room.

Miss Jane rose, this time in cathedral-like grandeur. Alas! she was a very weak-tempered woman. The cathedral brought forth a cat.

' What brings you back ? ' she cried. ' You are a disgrace to your sex: you are no lady; you are a shameless minx ! '

Muriel came close to her, her hand clutched in her pocket.

'Aunt,' she said, 'you are carrying this a little too far. Did you really suppose that I had gone at your command?'

'I certainly did; and I repeat it. Go!'

'When I leave this room, Frank goes with me. Supper will be served in a minute for him and me in my sitting-room.'

'Is it you or I that's dreaming, girl?'

'You have been dreaming, but you're wakening now. You thought you could mistress me; you can't.'

'If I can't mistress *you*, as you vulgarly say, we'll see whom the servants will obey.'

Miss Jane rang the bell violently.

Muriel's hand was again half-out of her pocket, but a whimsical expression came over her face, and she returned it.

'They shan't get the chance of disobeying you,' she said, going out of the room and holding the door shut. Her aunt tried to pull it open, but did not prosecute her attempt. It was too like a school-girl. She appealed to Frank tacitly. He shook his head. To tell the truth, the young man enjoyed it rather than not.

Shortly, a housemaid's voice was heard saying, 'Supper's just ready, Miss Muriel.'

The answer came, 'Very well; that's all,' and Muriel re-entered. She put her back against the door in a blaze of triumph, and said mock-heroically, 'No one shall leave this room till supper's served.'

Miss Jane was beaten, and Muriel had conquered without it; but now she held it out, and shook it open, remorselessly, her poor, little, crumpled letter. Her aunt, who had forgotten all about it, sank on the couch sobbing hysterically. Youth will exact the uttermost farthing, knowing not how it will need much mercy itself. The girl was punished there and then by a shade that passed over her lover's brow. She felt that he remembered the scene of the discovery, and contrasted it with this; but before she had decided what amends to make Lee entered the room. He looked about him, and immediately appeared to be in a tremendous passion, Miss Jane sat up; and Muriel, crossing the floor, took Frank's arm.

'Muriel,' said Lee, 'go to your room.'

She clung to Frank.

'I never bid twice,' and he pulled her away and swung her to the door.

'This is too much!' cried Frank, stepping towards Lee.

'Mr. Hay, I suppose. I shall speak with you immediately.'

Muriel was about to approach Frank again, but Lee pointed her sternly to the door. As before, in his presence, and by his conduct, she was utterly bewildered, and wandered out of the room as if she had lost her wits.

'Here's a change!' exclaimed Miss Jane, 'What a

disgraceful scene there has been here, brother! I apologise to myself for allowing my emotions to overcome me.'

'Leave us, please, Jane.'

'Certainly, Henry,' and as she went, she cast a withering look at Frank.

CHAPTER VI

LEE ENJOYS HIMSELF

LEE sat down behind the table and began to point a quill. Frank took a chair opposite him.

'Mr. Hay,' said Lee, 'we may as well come to the point at once. My daughter cannot marry you. I have chosen her a husband.'

'I am glad to come to the point at once,' said Frank. 'Miss Chartres bade me tell you that she will have no husband but me. She sends you this message: You may kill her, but you cannot force her to marry against her will.'

'I am sorry her message is so commonplace. It indicates that her novel-reading has not been eclectic, to say the least; and, which is of more importance to me, it lowers the tone of the present work. That, of course, you don't understand; but no matter. Force her to marry against her will? Surely not. *You* know, if *she* doesn't, that people never act against their wills. We will change her will, or kill it.'

'Which would be to kill her.'

'I'm not so sure of that. It will be an interesting experiment. I understand you to say that by the time my daughter's will has been conquered, her body must be so reduced that death will ensue. Now, I do not think so. What will you wager that she does not survive the subjugation of her will?'

There was a pause before Frank replied, which gave his answer an appearance of deliberation it did not possess. He was so astonished at the beaming satisfaction on Lee's face, utterly incompatible under any hypothesis he could think of, with the cold-blooded, heartless suggestion regarding Muriel, that words were denied him for a second or two. When they did come, slowly and vehemently, they had more reference to the character of the wagerer than the matter of the villanous bet.

' You are a scoundrel!'

Lee laid down the quill with which he had been dallying, and settled himself comfortably in his chair. He expected to derive great pleasure from this interview. Hitherto he had been dealing with women and servants; he was now to have a foeman worthy of his steel.

' I am a scoundrel,' he said, weighing each word. ' That is your position. Now, how will you defend it?'

The momentary blankness on Frank's face made Lee fear he had been too precipitate, and had routed the young man with this wholly unexpected turn, putting an end to the intellectual enjoyment he had anticipated. So when the blankness left Frank's face, the child-like happiness which dwelt in every line of

Lee's could only be matched by the pictured countenance of some rapt and smiling mediæval saint. The young man, concluding that he had to deal with what the world calls a 'character,' met him on his own ground.

'Your imperturbability under the accusation is the best proof, I think.' He said this mildly and collectedly, not wishing to give Lee the advantage of his coolness.

'A very fair answer,' said Lee. 'I shall allow you this stroke by way of compensation. Poor fellow, you will have a sore heart for a while, I imagine. You're not a fool, and you're good-looking. I think more of my daughter on your account.'

Lee resumed the quill, and began to write with a perfect assumption of unconcern. Frank stood up, put both hands on the table, leant forward a little, and delivered himself of a short speech. His blood was up, and he spoke very little above a whisper.

'Mr. Chartres, you have the right to control the actions of your daughter. You are going to abuse that right. I shall interfere. Your daughter loves me; you are going to force her from me; I shall do all I can to prevent you. I love your daughter; I shall stick at nothing to obtain her: Mr. Chartres, I shall succeed.'

The practical novelist positively trembled with delight.

'I like you, young man,' he cried; 'and I believe

you will improve. I think you will be unconsciously my best collaborateur. Both your character and Muriel's will be tested, illuminated, and strengthened for good or evil, in the course of this work, and that immediately. Who would write who has once tasted the pleasures of this new fiction! This is a foreign language to you. Some day I may teach you its whole secret. In the meantime regard me as a student of character, who, tired of books, of the dead subject, has taken to vivisection—vivisection of the soul. Well, sir, it is to be a duel, then. Good. I have a suspicion you imagine it is your bold bearing that makes me so placid. You are mistaken. It is my habit in opposition. I learnt it in the jungle, shooting tigers. My gun is always heavily loaded. I take a deliberate aim. If I shoot a tiger, it is killed; if a turtle-dove, it is blown to pieces. You comprehend.'

'Me, the turtle-dove; yes. And the bereaved mate will peck herself to death,' said Frank with considerable coolness.

'In a cage we can force her to live,' said Lee.

Frank had thought to meet Lee on his own ground, but found himself wholly at sea. He would strike out boldly till he touched land again.

'I am astonished,' he said, 'that a man like you, who seem to trample on conventionalities should arrogate to himself that absurd authority claimed by some fathers over the hands of their daughters.'

'And what if it were because parental jurisdiction

over marriage is becoming a thing of the past that I make myself absolute?'

'That would be very foolish,' said Frank, forgetting with whom he was dealing.

'That is no argument, my good sir,' came from Lee at once, and Frank saw his mistake.

'You see,' continued Lee, 'the idea of the parent is changing. The popular parent is the servant of his children. Now, whenever an idea, an opinion—a song, a faith, a show—becomes popular, I know at once it has some inherent weakness, some hollow lie; for the world is weak and false, and all kinds of froth and flame commend themselves to it. An opinion is like a jug of beer: the foaming head attracts the youth; the old toper blows it off.'

'You think yourself clever, but this is rank sophistry.'

'No argument again. Go away, Mr. Hay, and learn to do something besides assert. Come back and have a talk as soon as you really have something to say.'

Frank walked slowly to the door. He was endeavouring to estimate Lee. Did all fathers treat unsuitable candidates for their daughters' hands to such a dose of brusque philosophy? Surely not. Then, did all fathers returned from India with dark skins, and, presumably, no livers, behave in this fashion? He could not believe it. He returned to the charge.

'Why are you so ill-bred?' he asked.

'I am not ill-bred. Had I received you with any-thing but a downright refusal your hopes would have risen. Had I agreed with you in anything, you would have thought, "I may manage him yet." I have been kind to you. I have been most polite. I have not deceived you for an instant. Do not think that the suave manner is the sign of the kind heart. What is called politeness is, as you know, the commonest form of hypocrisy; courtesy has become etiquette, and the gentleman is the ghost of a dead chivalry.'

'You are a braggart as well as a sophist. You——'

'Go away till you learn to do other than assert and call names.'

'I will speak. You said a little while ago that when an opinion became popular, you, in effect, adopted its converse.'

'Too hard and fast; but go on.'

'Marriage is coming to be regarded more and more as a mere civil relation; you will, I have no doubt, look upon it as a sacred thing. If the heart does not go along with a holy ordinance, it is the blackest sin to take part in it. Will you play the devil to your own daughter?'

'Ah, this is better!' said Lee with glistening eyes. 'In the same way any marriage not consented to by the woman's father must be unholy also. Two evils you see.'

'Who can doubt which is the less?'

'Now you are the sophist. There is no less or

greater evil; it is all tarred with the same stick. But, to take a broader view. I firmly believe that marriages are made in heaven; therefore I should suppose, a marriage as ordained by heaven, happens once in fifty years, and it seems to me as likely that the decree of fate would be fulfilled in the father's choice as in the daughter's; and much more so when the father is a past master in the study of character.'

Frank was exasperated.

'Have you no heart?' he said.

The smile on Lee's face told him what a commonplace he had uttered. Smothering his emotion, he said, 'You teach me how to think and how to act. Marriages *are* made in heaven, and you were not married. If you had been you would have loved your daughter. A man of your no-principles must be answered as the fool is— according to his folly. And indeed you are a kind of fool, and a bad kind. I said before, thoughtlessly, that I would stick at nothing in endeavouring to make Miss Chartres my wife. Now I repeat it with full purpose.'

'Good,' said Lee, rubbing his hands. 'Still a little too much nicknaming, but, on the whole, good. You are a capital collaborateur. I have taught you how to think and act already. Are you not astonished at yourself? What would they think at your debating club of this talk of ours? If you like it, come back and have some more.'

Frank went to the door in silence, but returned again.

'Ah!' exclaimed Lee. ' "He often took leave, but was loath to depart!" What! Is it meant to be considered by me evidence of your determined spirit? Eh? Is it a dodge?'

'Ill-doers are ill-dreaders,' said Frank. 'I am not going to speak for myself, but for Muriel. You have talked of her as if she were a thing that you could turn to any use, and you have spoken of caging her. I perceive you to be most irrational and obstinate. I can imagine your going great lengths to obtain a desired end. Promise me that you will not use physical force in any——'

'I never make promises.'

'Then,' pursued Frank in a tone of entreaty that had mastered his voice to his great annoyance, for he felt that it was enjoyed like a sacrifice by the apparently infernal spirit whom he addressed—'I demand to know what weapons you will use. Will you employ force?'

'I am always armed to the teeth.'

'You mean you are unscrupulous.'

'Yes.'

'It is impossible to reason with you, I defy you. Why, you are an insolent, cold-blooded villain, and deserve a horsewhipping.'

'I will take an early opportunity of presenting you with a horsewhip to attempt the administration of one,' said Lee with perfect good humour.

'Let it be very soon,' said Frank, going, 'for when you are my father-in-law I will decline the offer.'

Lee rose to his feet. 'You wish this colloquy to end theatrically,' he said. 'I will disappoint you. You may marry my daughter, if you can.'

CHAPTER VII

THE UNEXPECTED

MURIEL had bribed the servant who should have shown Frank out to bring him to her sitting-room; and this was accomplished without observation. As he entered, Muriel's appearance astonished him. She looked superb in his eyes—flushed, bright, bold, a wonderful contrast to the haggard girl Lee had hurled from him half an hour before. The momentary defeated feeling was past. She now stood on her rights. No father or man should have treated her as Lee had done, and she replied by sticking to her purpose, and having Frank sup with her.

'Sit, sit,' she said. 'We'll not say a word about anything until we've supped—I mean about anything except the supper.'

They were both very hungry, and on the principle that promptitude in action is the best prayer for the success of any enterprise, dispensed with a grace. Truly, the good eater, if he masticate well, renders the best thanks. Frank and Muriel worshipped God heartily before the great mahogany altar of Britain—which was in this instance, a little one of walnut—

rapidly replacing the mercy of appetite by the mercy of satisfaction.

Meantime Lee had other visitors. Mr. Linty, the family lawyer, succeeded Frank almost immediately, and Miss Jane accompanied him into the library. Lee knew about him from some of the letters he had read. He was, however, wholly unprepared to enter into business with him; but pleasure he expected.

After the formal courtesies, the lawyer began. He was a sandy-haired, little, dry, old gentleman, and spoke very stiffly.

'Mr. Chartres,' he said, 'the intent with which I visit you to-day is to convey to you certain information which I think it my duty to let you have as soon as possible.'

' I am a man of business,' said Lee.

' Good, sir; very good. Mr. Chartres, an entailed estate is in a most delicate position, surrounded as it is with innumerable statutory provisions. It is doubtful whether you would be able, supposing you were so inclined, to make good a claim on Snell without proving the death of your brother Robert.'

Imagining that the lawyer had made a mistake in using Robert instead of William, and that there had been circumstances in connection with the death of the late proprietor which he had not learned; wishing, besides, to gain time, as this was the first intimation he had received of the estate being entailed, Lee said in a half-bantering tone, ' Well, you know, I never had a brother, Robert.

' O!' said the lawyer.

' Well,' began Miss Jane, but stopped short, not sure what to say or think.

Lee surpassed himself at this juncture. Not a feature of his face showed he was at a loss. He turned to Miss Jane and asked in a sort of parenthesis ' What were you going to say?'

' O!' said Miss Jane, ' I think, and I always told William, that although nothing has been heard of Robert for thirty years, he may still be alive. William said that he died to the family when he became a prodigal, and forbade his name to be mentioned. I thought that uncharitable.'

' Ay,' said Lee indifferently. ' Of course, I agreed with William.'

It was very successful.

' But,' said Mr. Linty, ' We *must* speak of him, for, if he is alive the estate is his. Do you know anything of him?'

' No,' said Lee; ' but as we have not heard of him for thirty years, we may reasonably suppose him dead.'

' By no means. That cannot even be taken as presumptive evidence. If there were seventy years from the birth of your brother there would be no difficulty, but if he is alive he will only be fifty-five. I am afraid the estate will require to be " hung up "—put into the hands of trustees.'

' Well, sir,' said Lee, rising, ' your contribution to

this work is wholly unexpected, but likely to produce most interesting complications. I am indeed much obliged to you. There is nothing original in it, but a missing heir is a very good thing to fall back on.'

The lawyer, supposing he had heard an elaborate, and, if so, certainly incomprehensible joke, laughed appreciatively. Miss Jane frowned and examined Lee all over with scorn and minuteness.

The latter continued. ' You must really excuse me just now. I only reached Snell House a few hours ago, and I am in no condition to discuss business. I suppose,' with a laugh, 'you won't turn us out . immediately.'

' By no means,' said Mr. Linty. ' In all likelihood there will be no need for that. I shall expect a visit from you to-morrow. Good evening.'

Miss Jane, who was a great friend of Mr. Linty's, left the library to see him to the door.

Lee's next visitor was of a different quality. He was an old man, very ill-dressed, the great size of his head, which was covered with thick white hair, being the most notable thing about him. Miss Jane introduced him, having met him at the door when she parted with the lawyer.

' This is Clacher, brother,' she said. ' You remember it was he who found William's body on the road.'

Lee did remember, as it had been mentioned in one of the letters he had read. Miss Jane informed Lee further under her breath, that Clacher was quite mad, although harmless, and that he got a living by begging in the disguise of a hawker. He had called often since the death of William, asking for the 'new Mr. Chartres.'

'I am very glad you have brought him to me,' said Lee. 'He may be useful.'

He then advanced to the old pedlar, and held out his hand, saying, 'How do you do, Mr. Clacher?'

Clacher emitted a chuckling noise, and darted glances at odd corners of the room—glances which, if it had been possible to enclose them, would have been found to resemble blind alleys, as they ran a certain distance into space and stopped without lighting on anything. Then he said in a hoarse, harsh voice, speaking to himself as much as to Lee, 'I'm gaun tae dae it Englified.'

He pulled himself up with all the appearance of a man about to make a lengthy statement; but instead of a speech he only succeeded in a pitiful pantomimic display. He could not remember what he had come to say. As if to stir up his dormant faculties he began rubbing his head with both hands, gathering his thick hair into shocks, and then scattering these asunder. While endeavouring to make hay of his hair in this manner, his little fierce eyes, like swivel-guns of exceedingly minute calibre, resumed firing their blank shots into space. Then, satisfied apparently that nothing could be done toward the tedding of his hair, he rubbed his shaved cheeks, beat his forehead and his breast, and tore at the fingers of both hands.

All at once he stood erect, and, as if he were resuming a train of thought, or a conversation, said, 'It's a wonnerfu' secret.'

'Indeed?' said Lee, quietly.

'Ay; for it can pit another in the deid man's shoes ye staun' in. But I was gaun tae dae it Englified. Ye micht check me when I gang wrang.'

'Check you when you go wrong?'

'That's it! "Go wrong"—no, "gang wrang." Keep me richt—right, will you, sir?'

'It's of no consequence to me, my good man,' replied Lee, whether you speak Englified as you call it, or not; but I'll keep you right if you like.'

'Thank you, thank you! But whaat——'

'What,' said Lee.

'Bide a wee, bide a wee!' cried Clacher, rubbing his hair.

'Ye see,' he continued, 'if I tak' time tae dae it Englified, I forget it. Whaat wis it I wis gaun tae dae Englified, and whaat for wis I gaun to dae it Englified? I canna' mind, I canna' mind.'

'Never mind, then,' said Lee, gently. 'You interest me as much as any character in the story. It seems indeed to be made to my hand, and I shall only require to mould it here and there in order to give it distinction.'

'Ye're mad, ye're mad!' cried Clacher, excitedly, shaking his big frowsy head, and seeing Lee for the first time, although his eyes had seemed fixed on him repeatedly.

'Poor fellow!' said Lee to Miss Jane, 'he thinks everybody mad but himself, like all lunatics.'

'Lunatics,' said Miss Jane, emphatically, 'are unerring judges of the lunacy of others.'

'I've heard that, too,' said Lee, ingenuously.

'My good friend,' he continued, addressing Clacher, 'we must really try and remember what and why it is to be done Englified. Come with me and you shall have something to eat and a glass of good wine. If that doesn't startle your memory I don't know what will.'

Miss Jane looked volumes, but only said, 'Henry, there never was a man so changed as you.'

'My dear Jane,' said Lee, 'in ten years—why, I might have become a lunatic too.'

As he crossed the hall with Clacher to the dining-room, a sound of laughter from upstairs struck on his ear. He stopped, and listened. It was repeated, and the laughing voices were Muriel's and another's. Entering the dining-room he hastily confided Clacher to the care of Briscoe and Dempster, who were discussing a bottle of port, and hurried away to Muriel's sitting-room. He went in without knocking, and another peal of laughter came to an early death. Frank and Muriel stood up as the door opened. She meant to fight; he recognised the falseness of their position, and felt, as he looked, exceedingly awkward.

'Father,' began Muriel, looking in Lee's direction, but past him, through the open door, 'you must not——'

She got no further; for she saw coming towards her room, in single file, Miss Jane, Dempster, Briscoe, and Clacher. It is pretty certain that none of these four persons knew exactly why they had come upstairs. Miss Jane probably expected some kind of scene to take place at which she might have an interest in assisting; Dempster followed her out of sheer stupidity; Briscoe came after Dempster because he was drunk; and Clacher after him because he was mad, and didn't know any better. When Miss Jane, arriving at the top of the staircase, saw Muriel's door open, she hesitated; but behind her there came such a motley procession that she had to go on. She stopped at the door; the others stood about her in a semi-circle, and the *tableau* was complete.

Lee, the only individual of the seven who was thoroughly collected, said, looking round him meditatively, 'The situation is turning out better than it promised to. After all, what more can we do either in writing fiction or creating it than follow an indication, and let the rest come.'

He then motioned Miss Jane aside and, taking Briscoe's hand, led him into the room. The maudlin gravity with which that worthy bore himself, combined with a remarkable bulging about the pockets, made him a very comic figure, and raised a smile even on Muriel's face. But Lee took one of her hands and put it in one of Briscoe's, saying, 'Muriel, this is your future husband.'

She turned very pale; and almost fainted, when a hazy smile struggled into Briscoe's slack mouth and dull eyes, and he attempted to kiss her. She broke from him with a half-suppressed exclamation of disgust, and would have thrown her arms round Frank; but Lee seized her, and handed her over to her aunt who had entered the room.

'Leave my house,' he then said to Frank, with a gesture of authority.

It was a peculiar position for the young man, and Lee watched him with intense interest. Frank walked to Muriel, kissed her on the cheek, whispered something in her ear, and then passed out through the little crowd at the door without looking to the right hand or the left.

'Very good!' exclaimed Lee. 'Perhaps that's the best thing he could have done.'

'But, Henry,' said Miss Jane, 'I think Mr. Dempster would like to marry Muriel.'

'Me!' shouted Dempster spirally. 'No; I assure you. My dear Miss Jane, I would as soon think of marrying you. Eh-ah—I mean well.'

Miss Jane's face quivered a second, but she said nothing, and left the room. Dempster, aghast at his dreadful mistake, followed her downstairs. Clacher, unable to make up his mind whether to stick by Briscoe or follow Dempster, sat down disconsolately on the top step, with his elbows on his knees and his head between his hands. Lee also went out, signing to Briscoe to follow him. Then Lee locked Muriel into her room, and putting the key in his pocket, took Briscoe and Clacher to the library with him.

It was half-past nine when Muriel found herself a prisoner; and Frank had whispered that he would wait for her all night at the low wall.

CHAPTER VIII

BRISCOE SEES THINGS IN A NEW LIGHT

FOOD and drink were provided for Clacher in the library. It was a very large room, and he sat at a little table in the corner, out of hearing of the low tones in which Briscoe and Lee conversed.

Lee was exceedingly angry at Briscoe for having got tipsy, and rated him severely, getting no response, however, save laughter or a drunken 'You shut up.' At last, losing patience, he dashed a tumbler of water in the drunken man's face. Briscoe rose to strike; but Lee gave him another tumbler, and while he was still rubbing the water out of his eyes, a third, which knocked him down into his chair again, pretty well sobered and very surly. Lee was a man of great physical strength, and although on several occasions Briscoe had been able to control his will, a single bout at fisticuffs had shown, once for all, who was master in that branch of dialectic.

'My dear Briscoe,' said Lee, handing him his handkerchief to help to dry himself, 'this is really too bad of you. Do you think I don't know the meaning of those stuffed pockets of yours? You've been helping yourself, forgetting altogether the work of art in which we are engaged.'

'Heaven helps those that help themselves,' growled Briscoe, still a little maudlin and very crusty.

'A very good proverb indeed; but it has always seemed to me to require a gloss, as, say, "Help yourself, and Heaven will develop heroic qualities in you by opposing you." So you see I am interfering with you to give your acts a higher tone. You'll have to empty out your pockets, my boy. Nobody need know; and, if they should, kleptomania is quite genteel.'

'Now, look here,' said Briscoe : ' I'm not fit for this almighty art of yours. By Jove, when I think of where I am, and what we're up to, I can hardly believe it's me ! Just you give me as much money as you can, and let me slope quietly, and you'll get on far better without me. I never could grease myself and worm through the tight places—get through the world, as folks say; and I tell you it would be far better for you if I were away.'

'Briscoe, I have always admired your independent character,' said Lee. 'Neither can I get through the world; but there's another method which equally insures success, and that is, to transcend the world : death by starvation is then itself a glorious triumph— the triumph of the idea. I know what I mean, and, though I were to explain till doomsday, you wouldn't, so it don't matter. You will confer a lasting benefit on the world if you stay and help with the work in which I am engaged. It is a glorious labour, apart from its artistic merit; for it is raising the tone of everybody about me. It is just what these people needed, especially Muriel and Frank—the dash of bitter that strengthens the sweet, the need for rebellion that wakens the soul, the spur that drives natures roughshod over convention, the——'

'Draw it mild,' interposed Briscoe sneeringly. 'To-morrow, or maybe to-night, Caroline will be down with the real man, and what will you do then?'

'I long for their arrival. That will be the great scene.'

'What'll you do?'

'Well, murder I merely glanced at. To turn them out of the house as impostors, though a simple solution of the matter for a short time, would only stave off a final settlement. This is what I intend: to shut up Chartres in one of the rooms, pinioned, and, if necessary, gagged, as a dangerous lunatic, until I can have him removed to a private asylum, which will be a matter of only a few hours; and, once there, we are safer than if he were in the grave.'

'How will you manage that?'

'The simplest thing in the world. You can't have read many novels or you wouldn't ask. Besides the novels, however, I have studied the lunacy laws; and I could put you, Briscoe—sensible, hard-headed fellow as you are—into an asylum to-morrow, and defy the world to take you out!'

'By Jove, there's a chance here!' said Briscoe. 'Damn it, man, banish your dreams, and do the thing as a downright piece of the finest villainy ever perpetrated.'

'I haven't the least objection, my dear Briscoe, that you should be a villain. There's not one, at present, in the work, and if you choose, still collaborating with me, to adopt such a *rôle*, I shall be very glad indeed.'

'I'll do it,' said Briscoe, rising. 'I'll go off to Glasgow and prepare the whole thing for to-morrow early.'

'The last train from Greenock left some time ago.'

'What! is it so late as that?'

'Yes; but you can go off to-morrow before breakfast.'

'Very well. But we're going to do this, mind! No shamming—no artistic flourishes—upright, downright villainy!'

'On your part, certainly.'

'And I'm to marry Muriel?'

'Oh, you must see that is impossible. The girl will fight to the death against it. Besides, it would be thoroughly inartistic. No, no. My intention is to bring about an elopement; and then to discover that you are Frank's father. You see? You're old enough. He's only twenty-two, and you're over forty. The invention of antecedents and the getting up evidence will be most engrossing. Of course I'll intercept these young people, and drive them to the very last resource. It will do them any amount of good.'

Briscoe put up his hand warningly, and Lee turned his head and saw Clacher standing behind him.

'Ah! my good friend,' he said, 'have you had enough?'

'Ay,' said Clacher.

'Do you remember what it is you want to do "Englified"?'

'No—yet.'

'Do you think you'll remember soon?'

'Mebbe, if ye'll let me alone, and gie me some mair drink. Whusky.'

'Certainly,' said Lee, rising. 'You can have this room to yourself, and I shall send you whiskey.'

'I think I'll go to bed,' said Briscoe. 'I'm very tired; and I'll have an early start to-morrow.'

'Come out and smoke a cigar with me first,' said Lee. And then in a whisper, 'I want you to help me. They may arrive any moment.'

'Of course,' replied Briscoe, in the same tone, clenching his fists. 'I forgot that.'

So Clacher was left with a decanter of whiskey; and as soon as he was alone he pulled from his breast-pocket a dirty letter, which he read and re-read, and thought over and got madder about: and he always took the other glass of whiskey, muttering to himself, 'I canna' mind, I canna' mind.'

CHAPTER IX

DEMPSTER APOLOGISES

WHILE Briscoe was being sobered in the library a remarkable scene transacted itself in the dining-room between Miss Jane and Dempster. The outraged lady settled herself in an easy chair with a book; but the offender entered before she had time to read six lines. He approached her on tip-toe, and, a spring seeming to give way somewhere within him, he came down plump on one knee, as if he had been a puppet, and burst out woefully ' Eh-ah ! ' like an escape of saw-dust.

Miss Jane ignored him, and pressed open her book, which was new and stiff.

Dempster cleared his throat of the saw-dust, and with drooping head, his left hand on his left knee and his right arm hanging limp, whispered, just above his breath, ' Miss Chartres, you see before you a miserable being.'

' I don't; I'm not looking,' said the lady sharply, disconcerting Dempster terribly.

' If you would look you would see me,' he said nervously, as several watch-springs seemed to break out of bounds in various parts of his anatomy.

Miss Jane looked over the top of her book. She saw him collapsed before her with abased eyes, and was satisfied. So she hid her face again, smiling, and said coldly, 'I have seen you.'

'Have you?' said Dempster, going off, as it were accidentally, like a gun; 'I'm very glad: for I would have had no rest of mind or body if you hadn't looked at me. I would have gone about like a hen that had lost her—I mean——'

'Well, and say ill, Mr. Dempster,' said Miss Jane, unable to resist the chance which she had long desired to take. 'These kind of people often make more mischief than ill-doers,' she added.

This overwhelmed Dempster. Down he came on the other knee, and, clasping both hands, called out in serpentine anguish, and without a stammer, 'Why are you so hard on me? The moment I made that unfortunate remark about marrying you, the earth, the sun, my wealth, and life and death were to me no more than they are to a poor man. I assure you, I assure you—I don't exaggerate; and I beg you, I implore you to forgive me.'

'Rise, Mr. Dempster,' said Miss Jane with a slight return of graciousness. 'There is really nothing to forgive.'

Some automatic winding-up process began within him and would soon have brought him to his feet with a bound, but Miss Jane's reply to his 'And we will be friends as we were before?' made him all run down again; for the lady said, 'That can hardly be. Though mistakes may not require forgiveness, they cannot always be forgotten. But rise, please.'

'I'll not rise till you forget,' said Dempster with pitiful resignation, his various members barely hanging together. The poor fellow was in deader earnest than even Miss Jane supposed, as will shortly appear.

'But I cannot forget,' said the lady. 'Thought is free, and self-willed besides, Mr. Dempster.'

He clasped his hands again, and in a succession of spasms ejaculated, 'You are the only woman whose society I have any comfort in. You understand me; and your advice is always good, and—eh—ah—agreeable. You never snub me—at least not often, and not without good reason—like younger, like thoughtless hoydens. If you won't forget and be friends with me again, I don't know whatever I'm to do. I have nothing at all to think of now Muriel has rejected me; and I'll have nobody I can talk to with any frankness if you go on remembering.'

Miss Jane's blood, which was not by any means a meagre decoction, but on the contrary rich and sweet enough yet, tingled to her finger ends. This man actually needed her! She laid aside her book, leant forward a little, resting her hands neatly in her lap. There was no smile, but she looked with a gentle earnestness, and the tang was gone from her tongue.

'How am I to forget?' she said. 'Tell me that, and I'll try. I suppose *you* have not forgotten what you said—very bitter words for any woman to digest. You would as soon think of marrying me as of marrying a young hoyden, who, from what I can make out, had just rejected you with insult; and the tone of voice—the tone of voice! But rise, Mr. Dempster.'

'I won't,' he said, looking her right in the face, and wondering that he had never noticed before how silky her brown hair was, and how kindly her brown eyes. 'I won't. Forget and then I'll rise.'

'How can I forget?' softly.

'Just as easily as I can rise. The mind is like legs; it can be bent and unbent.'

Now Miss Jane was not very much of a prude; but Dempster was becoming too confident. He must be brought low again. So she lifted her book and said 'Shocking!'

'I beg your pardon,' he cried, vexed at finding the stumbling-block, which he had nearly rolled up to the top and kicked over the other side out of sight for ever, down at the bottom of the hill again. 'I didn't mean to say,' trying to twist his fingers into a hay-band, 'that your mind was like my legs—oh dear me! I've put both feet in it now!'

Miss Jane hid her face completely, but it was to conceal a smile.

Dempster smoothed his cheeks with both hands and held his head for a second or two, all of him gathered up in a more powerful effort to think than he had ever made in his life before.

'What can I do to make you forget?' he muttered.

'Ah!' he cried, after a second, pulling the book from Miss Jane's face as a child might have done, 'I think I'm going to have an idea.'

'You don't mean to say so!' said Miss Jane, leaning forward again in the same neat, pleasant way, with a laugh that was almost girlish.

'Yes, I believe I am,' said Dempster, sitting down on the calves of his legs with his hands on his knees, and looking up trustfully, like something in india-rubber.

'If I were to say,' he enunciated slowly, 'something contradicting emphatically what you can't at present forget, you might—eh—ah—forget?'

'Yes.'

He had been about a foot from her, and he now scraped along the ground on his knees until he almost touched hers.

'You might try to say something of that kind,' she said, blushing, and with a little gasp. Now that it seemed to be coming she was put out; but, like a brave woman having her last chance, she kept her position and smiled encouragingly.

'Might I? Oh, thank you!' he cried with effusion.

Then he knitted his brows and rubbed his head. His serpentine faculty was in abeyance—these involuntaries of his had to cease in order that he might once in his life attempt to think.

As for Miss Jane, she was mistaken in imagining

that he had the least notion of making love to her. He valued her only as a friend, and had splashed into the quicksand of a proposal of marriage without knowing it. She thought, however, that he only needed a touch to make him bury himself, like a flounder, head over ears in a declaration of love and an offer of his hand and heart; so she gave him that touch softly and sweetly.

'You said,' quoth she, 'with the utmost disdain, that you would as soon think of marrying me as my insolent niece.'

'I did, I did. Can you help me to contradict it emphatically?'

'I'm afraid not—dear Mr. Dempster.'

'Eh?' said he. 'Thank you.'

He felt dimly that there was something in the air—dimly, as protoplasm may feel its existence.

'Ah!' he cried. 'Here's a kind of notion. I wonder if it's an idea. Would it do to say, in order to make you forget, just the opposite of what I said? You see—you understand—something like this, meaning—of course, you know what I mean—nothing more, you know—eh—ah!—suppose I say, "I would far rather marry you than Muriel." Is that—emphatic enough?'

Miss Jane bent forward, and put her head on his left shoulder, and her hand on his right.

'Mr. Dempster!' she said. 'Alec!' she sighed.

'Eh?—eh—ah!'—and he had to hold her—to clutch her, to save himself from falling.

'I'm the happiest woman in the world.'

'I'm—I'm very glad of it.'

'I never loved anybody before,' she said, so sweetly that Dempster wondered.

Then she buried her face in his neck, she did, the stupid, soft-hearted creature, and whispered, 'Oh, the torture of wooing you for Muriel! But now I have my reward!'

And she did think this as she said it, although it had never occurred to her before.

'Yes,' said Dempster, feeling that the pause must be filled up somehow. 'Of course,' he added, making a half-hearted attempt to force her back into her chair, which she mistook for a caress, 'I only suggested the contradiction. I did not——'

But her eyes were shut, and her brain too.

'I adore your modesty,' she whispered. 'Trust me, trust me. I will love you till death.'

'I'm completely stumped,' exclaimed Dempster.

'Poor dear!' said Miss Jane, mistaking. And, indeed it was pardonable, Dempster's metaphors being usually marked by a *curiosa infelicitas.*

Here the door opened briskly and Mrs. Cherry, the housekeeper, burst into the room.

'Losh me! Miss Chartres!' she cried, as the pair scrambled to their feet.

'Mrs. Cherry,' said Miss Jane, with great presence of mind, in spite of a distinct tremor in her voice, 'since you have seen, I may as well tell you. Mr.

Dempster is going to marry me. But why did you come in without knocking, and what do you want?'

Mrs. Cherry made a dreadful mess of her story. It will be clearer to the reader in a form different from that which she gave to it.

The housekeeper's room was on the ground floor, and directly under Muriel's sitting-room. About half-past nine Mrs. Cherry's gossip, Mrs. Shaw, dropped in for a chat. These two good women were widows of fifty, and whatever their talk began with, it usually ended in laudation of their sainted husbands. The crack reached that stage about ten o'clock on the night of our story, and Mrs. Shaw's panegyric was soon in full blast.

'Maister Shaw,' she said, twiddling her thumbs, 'wis a fine man. The cliverest, godliest, brawest Christian, an' a gentleman though he merrit me. He could write, ay, an' coont, mind ye, for a' the warl' as weel as ony bairn o' fourteen in thae' days when a' body's brats gang to the schule. An' for readin'— losh, wumman!—he would sit glowerin' at a pipper a nicht wi' the interestedest look in his een— sae dwamt-like that ye wad hae' thocht he didna' ken a word.'

'What's that?' said Mrs. Cherry, starting in her chair.

'What's what?' said Mrs. Shaw.

'I thocht I heard a scart at the windy, an' somethin' gie a saft thump on the gravel.'

'Ne'er a bit o't. Some maukin loupin' alang, or mebbe a rotten or a moosie clawin' in the wa' tae let us ken it's time we were beddit, and the hoose quate, for it tae come oot an' pike the crumbs on the flare, an toast its bit broon back in the ase. I mind fine sitting at oor ingle ae Januwar nicht wi' Maister Shaw. He had a pipper, an' I was knittin'. There was nae soond but the wag-at-the-wa' tick-tickin', like an artifeecial cricket with the busiest, couthiest birr, an' my wairs gaun clickaty-click, when I heard a cheep, cheep. Maister Shaw an' me lookit up thegither, an' there we saw, sittin' on the bar fornent the emp'y side—for the chimbley was that big we aye keepit a fire in the half o't only—the gauciest, birkiest, sleekest wratch o' a moose, cockin' its roon' pukit lugs, an' keekin' by the corners o' naethin' wi' its bit pints o' een. By-an'-bye it gied anither chirp, an' syne we heard a kin' o' a smo'ored cheepin' at the back o' the lum; an' in a gliflin' seeven wee bonny moosikies happit oot a hole that naebody wad hae' thocht o' bein' there, an' crooched in a raw, winkin' on their minnie. I lookit at Maister Shaw, an' he turn't up his een like a deid blaeck in the dumfooderdest way; an' his pipper gied the gentiest sough o' a rooshle; an' whan we lookit at the grate again we just got a glint o' the wairy tail o' the big moose weekin' intae its hole. But lord hae' mercy! What's that?'

'I tell't ye!' quoth Mrs. Cherry.

'Gosh me! There it's again!'

Twice a sound similar to that which had first startled Mrs. Cherry was repeated—a slight swish past the window, and a flop on the gravel.

The two old ladies sat with their hands clasped and their mouths open. Neither of them had the courage to pull up the blind, and watch if on a third repetition the sound should be accompanied by any sight. In a few seconds a louder, harder thud, preceded by no rubbing on the window, and followed by a noise as of some one running on the gravel, appalled the two old dames. Screaming, they flew to the kitchen, where Mrs. Cherry left her friend, and hurrying to the dining-room, in her fright threw open the door without announcing herself, and interrupted so interesting a *tête-à-tête*.

Miss Jane, by dint of interrogation and remorseless interruption, which sometimes failed in its object—that of restoring to Mrs. Cherry the thread of her story—at length understood, discarding a vast quantity of irrelevant information, that the two women had been frightened by strange noises at the window of the housekeeper's room. Shrewdly guessing as to its cause, she was proceeding with Dempster to institute a formal investigation into the mystery, when a much more incomprehensible affair met her in the hall.

This is what she saw : Lee and Briscoe carrying the body of a man—who might be dead or unconscious, and whose face was covered with a handkerchief—and followed by a tall comely woman, sobbing bitterly. They passed upstairs. Miss Jane, Dempster, and the housekeeper were still standing at the door of the dining-room, amazed and silent, when Lee came down.

'You must allow this to pass unquestioned at present,' he said loftily. 'It is a very serious and sorrowful matter, and I would prefer to explain it to-morrow.'

'Very well, Henry,' said Miss Jane, even more loftily, 'you know your own affairs best. By-the-bye,' she added, as if it were a matter of course, 'from what Mrs. Cherry tells me, I think Muriel has jumped out of the window.'

'By Jove! Where should she go?'

'To the north wall, of course.'

'To be sure.'

Snatching a riding-whip from a rack, he strode to the door, but turned and said, 'This must be left entirely to me—entirely,' he repeated as Miss Jane began to remonstrate.

She was much huffed, but withdrew into the dining-room with Dempster, and the housekeeper returned to her room.

Lee had received his first check. Hitherto everybody and everything had obeyed him; but now Briscoe had spoiled part of his plan. Briscoe's courage had soon ebbed in the coolness of the night-air, and, instead of allowing the scene to take place which Lee wished in order to justify him in having Chartres bound and gagged as a madman, he had made the latter insensible the moment he stepped out of the cab which had driven him and Caroline from Greenock. This was done with chloroform, a bottle of which he had found while rummaging through the bedroom assigned to him. Caroline he had quieted by assuring her that if she said one word of betrayal he would at once put an end to Chartres' life—a threat, which, having regard to what had already taken place, she did not care to brave.

In this way Briscoe had taken the lead, reducing Lee to the necessity of acting along with him for the nonce.

CHAPTER X

THE NIGHT BREEZE

FRANK sat on the north wall watching the moon through the leaves. Her light was faint, for the skirts of the day still swept the west. He had watched her for half an hour—the pale crescent, which even in that short time had seemed to wane, as her light waxed and her horns grew keener on the night's front—the high forlorn hope of heaven's host that could not all that month drive out the day. He sat under the close silence of the elm, among whose leaves there crept the faint, veiled murmur of the seaboard, fingered by the brooding surges as they beat out their slow, uncertain, soft-swelling music. Now and again there came, twining among the mellow notes of the water, from some far field the corncrake's brazen call, and made the gold ring stronger. These sounds, the pale moonlight, the night, and the idea of Muriel, possessed him to the exclusion of thought. Passion rendered him impassive, and he waited without impatience. Slowly pealing from the tower in Gourock, ten strokes told the hour. A crackling twig, a footstep, a rustle, and Muriel was beside him.

Nothing was said till she had recovered her breath; then her voice, tuned unconsciously to the rippling accompaniment of the waves, whispered clear, 'When you had gone, my father locked me in my room. The thought of waiting-and-waiting here all night would soon have made me mad, so I got out by the window. I threw out a cushion, and then I was frightened. But after a little my courage came back again, and then I threw over two more, and dropped down quite soft. I don't know whether any one saw or heard me; but you wanted me, and I'm here. See, I tore my dress.'

He kissed her dress.

'You must not enter your father's house again,' he said.

Her breath came quick; she took his arm, and looked at him intently.

'Do you know your father?' he asked.

'He is difficult; but I am beginning to.'

'Then you will understand why his house is not for you.'

She had only a look with which to answer, and he did not think it satisfactory.

'Tell me,' he said, 'do you understand?'

'No; I do not. My father wants me to marry a stranger, but he cannot make me.'

'Then you do not know him. He has no scruples; he will do anything.'

'What can he have said to impress you so?'

'He said enough to show me he has no conscience, and that he looks on you as a mere puppet.'

Muriel felt as if the world were breaking up on all sides. What strange new things the day had brought forth; and, to crown them, flight from home seemed imminent! She pressed to her side Frank's arm, and with her disengaged hand smoothed the collar of his coat and fastened the top button, all the while looking wistfully at his set face. The ears of both were ringing with their own blood, or they would have heard a movement among the branches; for at that moment Lee reached the elm. His intention was to interrupt at once, and get back to the ravelled skein in the house; but the vision of the two lovers solaced his artistic sense; he was so near that he could hear their whispers. Shall not an artist take delight in his own work? Chance would help him, as it had done, manfully. He would watch this scene out. Surely he held the strings; and these, his daintiest puppets, he must see them play their best.

'You must come away with me,' said Frank hoarsely. 'See, I would have you what is called elope, and I am scrupulous. I do not know if such an action can be justified by our position even to ourselves. Your father has no scruples. Conceive what he will do.'

Two incidents flashed into Muriel's mind; the elopement of one former schoolmate, and the forced marriage of another; both ending in death by heartbreak of the young wives. She was angry at herself that these should have occurred to her. Frank and she!—they were apart from the world. Yet she whispered, ‘You surely exaggerate.’

‘No; I do not,’ he said. ‘Come with me, just now. We are in Scotland. I will marry you to-night—regularly, to-morrow. You needn’t fear: I have plenty of money.’

‘O Frank!’ she cried reproachfully, ‘if I thought my marrying you depended on running off just now, I would go although you hadn’t a penny.’

‘It does, it does. Step on the wall, and I will help you down.’

This command, and the action which accompanied it, roused her. She had not fully realised the purpose that made his pleading so earnest, until he seized her quickly, and lifted her towards the wall.

Lee grasped his whip tightly, and was ready for a spring.

‘Put me down,’ said Muriel.

Frank hesitated for a moment. It came into his brain to profess a misunderstanding of her meaning, and lift her over; but looking in her eyes he blushed with shame at the imagination of such a deceit. When she was free she seated herself at the root of the tree, and clasped her knees, gazing at vacancy. She sat for a full minute. He did not interrupt her meditation. He scarcely thought that she had divined his momentary impulse. Nevertheless, he felt as if she had, and punished himself by remaining silent and apart. He watched her face. It was a sweet perplexity. He chafed to think that he could not resolve her difficulty.

At length her brow cleared. She rose and went to the wall. She looked up and down the road and over her shoulder enchantingly. Then she lifted her skirts over the wall and sat with her back to Frank. In a second she turned round, and dropped with a little laugh into the road. He sprang after her, and seized her hand. Leo approached the wall, but still kept himself concealed.

' Muriel ! ' Frank whispered breathlessly.

' Frank,' she said, giving him her hand, ' I will do what you think right. That's what I meant by coming over the wall—I am in your hands. But first I will tell you what I think. My father wishes me to marry his friend. That is all we know at present. If the time should come when I must either obey my father or fly with you, you know what I would do. But I do not see that that time can ever come.'

' Yes,' said he. ' But if your father should give you this alternative—either to marry his friend or remain single ? '

' I was coming to that, although it seems too ridiculous to be likely. Well, we would elope.'

There was silence for several seconds. Unwittingly they had to accustom themselves to the changed environment, although the difference was slight. Their natures were so quickened, so responsive, that soon a perfect accord existed between them and the latticeless moonbeams, the wide, open night, and the undeadened music of the surges. They crossed the road in order to be wholly free of the shade of the elm, not thinking why they did so. Lee, on his knees behind the wall, watched them with glowing eyes.

At length Frank said, 'You are here; you are beautiful; you are hopeful; and you make me hopeful too. I have dreamt so long of having you that I cannot, with you beside me, imagine our not being married. But I force myself to remember your father's determined tone, his cold-blooded sophistries. I heard the worst, most insolent, most foul, most damnable——'

'Frank!'

'Most foolish talk fall from your father's lips about you, Muriel. It is horrible to talk to you in this way; but I tremble when I think of your being left to your father's tender mercies. Listen. I have challenged him to keep you from me, and he has accepted the challenge. I regret it now. He said that he would use every means; that he was always armed to the teeth; so I resolved at once to run away with you, and dared him. I have been rash—or should I save you in spite of yourself?'

She looked at the ground, working with both hands at the buttons of her dress. He had described her mental condition as well as his own. His presence had cast into the shade the recollection of her talk with Lee. The threat contained in what Lee had said about 'coming to the point and never returning to it' now assumed portentous shape in her fancy, quickened by Frank's forebodings; and the happy, trustful, resolved expression which her face had worn when she climbed over the wall gave place to one of wretched doubt.

Frank, watching her closely, would not take advantage of her wavering mood, and refrained from word or action. His whole endeavour had been to overcome her repugnance to an elopement; yet when it was shaken, he made no attempt to improve the occasion. He felt that to do so would be like striking a man when he is down. What he aimed at was to make her throw him the reins and be passive. This she had seemed to do when she went over the wall, but the surrender had not been absolute.

'I am puzzled,' she said hastily, knitting her brows at the moon. 'I cannot decide. I shall tell you how I am thinking, and then, perhaps, I shall find out what it is right to think. It is clearer to think aloud. Elopement! It is a bad, vulgar thing. It would be in all the papers—forgive me, love! I am thinking that way. I can't help it. People would joke about it as long as we lived. My father would never forgive me. Frank— Frank Hay! I love him, and he loves me. My father doesn't love me. Frank wants me to elope. What would it matter about newspapers and society when we were married? I am a foolish girl. It always comes round to this: would it be right just now? Could it ever be right? Here I am in the road. You must decide.'

This was spoken with extraordinary emphasis, and at a great rate of speed; and when it was done the trouble passed off her face. It settled on his. He pushed his hat from his forehead, thrust his hands into his pockets, confronting her, and said, 'I hoped for this, and intended to carry you off in triumph. Whatever withholds me, I cannot.'

Vacillation is not always the sign of a weak nature. The wind veers round the compass, and then the gale sets in steadily. Frank had never been on such a high sea of moral difficulty before. He had some crew of principles; but they were not able-bodied, having slept for the most part through the plain sailing of his life. When the storm came the drowsy helmsman, Conscience, started up rubbing his blinking eyes; and Will, the captain, had no order to give.

He climbed the wall, and held down his hands to Muriel. She put one foot in a little hole; he pulled her up; and they were again under the elm, Lee barely escaping discovery.

Now, just at the instant Frank gave Muriel his hands, and she clambered up the wall with the grace of a wild thing and the necessary free movements; just when her panting body was in his arms, and her breath upon his face, there came out of the south one long, gentle, trembling, warm sigh, bearing a burden of subtle odour from the half-reaped hayfields, and making the trees shiver with delight through all their happy branches, and the sap swell and trickle to the very tips of the downiest twigs. It was Summer kissing Nature in the night. Frank and Muriel were caught in the contagion. Passion whirled round their hearts that had been held by consciences alike inexperienced, and the poor helmsmen were overset. Their blood rattled along their veins like uncontrolled rudder-chains. He lifted her over; and, taking her in his arms again when he joined her in the road, started to carry her. They would be married that night.

A long shadow thrown suddenly across the road arrested him, and immediately a tall figure stood up in the moonlight. He set Muriel on her feet behind him, and faced Lee.

'Mr. Chartres!' he exclaimed hoarsely.

'You wished,' said Lee, handing him the riding-whip, 'for an opportunity to horsewhip me.'

'Villain!' cried Frank savagely, seizing the whip. He raised it to strike. His rage was simply that of a foiled animal.

'Haven't you got over that bad habit of calling names yet?' said Lee with a smile, as he caught the hand that held the descending whip. Frank shifted it to the other hand, which Lee grasped as quickly. Thus Lee held by the wrist a hand of Frank's in each of his.

Muriel uttered a little scream and fell on her knees. She kept her eyes fixed on the whip. It jerked about overhead for a few seconds and fell to the ground. Then she looked at the men. Their arms were locked round each other. They staggered about and knocked against the wall. She heard them breathing hard. She held her own breath. She had scarcely begun to think what would be the upshot when Frank fell with a thud on his back, and Lee stood over him whip in hand.

'You have killed him!' she screamed, starting to her feet, and rushing to her prostrate lover.

'Hardly,' said Lee, throwing the whip away, rather ostentatiously, as he stepped aside to let Frank rise. He got up looking very unheroic; indeed, decidedly sheepish. Lee folded his arms, paler, if anything, than the other, and said, 'I won't ask you to try another fall. I think I am just twice as strong as you. I mean this to be a lesson. If you are wise, you will not attempt to struggle with me in anything.'

Frank stood with his eyes fixed on the ground, his self-esteem had fallen with his body; Muriel had seen him beaten.

Lee, resting a hand on Muriel's shoulder, and forcing her to stand beside him when she shrank away, said gaily, 'She is really a splendid girl, this daughter of mine. How handsome she looks just now! You must be chagrined horribly when you think that you almost had her. My dear boy, I pity you sincerely. I don't know exactly what course you should follow. It would be very striking, certainly, if you were to go off and drown yourself at once; but I don't think you'll do that. For myself I would prefer that you shouldn't. I like you too well, and hope that you will continue to play a part in our story.   Perhaps you might take to drink. That's a good idea. Go in for dissipation; there's nothing like it for the cure of romance. Unworldly diseases need worldly remedies. And yet that's too common, especially with lady novelists. I believe you'll hit on some bright course of your own, for you're a capital collaborateur. I must thank you and Muriel for this scene. I've witnessed it all. Oh, you needn't be ashamed!' for Frank shut his eyes tightly, and Muriel hid her face in her hands. 'You're most delightful young people. The way you answered at once to that soft, warm gust charmed me, charmed me. I understand it all perfectly. I also am at one with nature. Well, good night. Come, Muriel.'

Taking her hand he moved toward the wall. She looked over her shoulder to catch a glance from Frank, but his eyes were still fixed on the ground, and he stood motionless. Quick as a fawn she leapt from Lee's side, and throwing her arms round Frank's neck, cried out loud in a tone mingled of anguish and pity and passion, 'I love you!' and he, reanimated by that shout, whispered as Lee snatched her away, 'I'll watch here all night.' That gave her new hope too. She would come to him by some means or other; and she felt so contented as Lee helped her over the wall, and led her in silence to the house, that she wondered at herself.

CHAPTER XI

CONCLUSION

It was nearly eleven o'clock.   Lee, Briscoe, Miss Jane, Dempster and Muriel were all in the dining-room, and Dempster was making a speech.   It will possibly never be known whether Miss Jane put him up to it or not; if she did she regretted it before he was half done.

'Ladies and gentlemen,' he began, with turgid tongue and desiccated throat, ' you are surprised that I should wish at this late hour to detain you with anything in the shape of a formal speech, however informal it may be.'   The introductory sentence had been prepared.   'But,' he continued, staunching a wriggle, ' I— I have something to say.   Mr. Chartres, I am neither a Communist nor a Nihilist '—this was to have been a side flourish, but out it came first—' still I would like to remark, in reference to a talk we had this afternoon, that I am of opinion that, if fortunes were things to be inherited by everybody, it might on the whole be better —eh—ah—or worse for society, taking into consideration the fact that wealth produces idleness, and idleness folly, and—eh—ah—sin, it might be better that most people should have to make their fortunes.   Eh—ah—I am overwhelmed with a feeling such as one experiences when one gets something one didn't expect. Comfort, Mr. Chartres, is the greatest necessity of existence—I mean that to be comfortable is always of the greatest consequence, indeed, I may say, the very backbone—eh—ah—of comfort.'

Now there is never the remotest necessity for speech-making, at least in private, although it is daily perpetrated, and unfailingly by wholly incompetent parties. It is like singing in this respect; only those who cannot care to perform. Human nature will never get past it; for there is a law which ordains that whatever one is unfit for must be attempted, especially out of season. What one can't do is the all-important thing. So Dempster reeled on, undeterred by the blank looks of his auditors, and an ominous sparkle in Miss Jane's eye—his body a mere thoroughfare of uninterrupted transmigration for the spirits of all things that crawl and squirm and twist and wriggle.

'And I am now, I am happy to say, exceedingly comfortable. After Muriel refused me I was like a ship in a storm, and so I put into the first port—eh—ah—I mean that I have found a comfortable haven, and I am sure Jane will make a very good wife.'

Amazement stared from every eye, including Miss Jane's. She tried to simper in a dignified manner—but what was the man saying?

'She is like old wine—eh—ah '—he felt Miss Jane's eyes scorching him like burning-glasses. 'The difference between our ages—eh—ah— ' he was now perspiring freely. 'The disadvantage of marrying a girl like Muriel is, that when she grows old'—he made a little halt here, but he was too far gone to draw back ; over he went, head first—'when she grows old one would miss her beauty. The great advantage is that one can never miss what has never been there, and—I'll not be interrupted!' mopping his head, and gyrating fiercely ; but not daring to meet again Miss Jane's eye, one full glance of which had been more than enough.

'There's nobody interrupting you, my dear Mr. Dempster,' said Lee. ' But is it true that you are going to marry my sister ?'

'It is—I am !' defiantly, as if he were challenging himself to take so much as one step in an opposite direction.

' I'm very glad. An episode of this kind is refreshing. So unlikely too! One daren't have introduced it into written fiction ; but here it has cropped up most beautifully in our little creation. Really, I am much obliged to you both. Now you must allow me to go upstairs and attend to the matters there.'

As soon as Lee had reached the house with Muriel he had gone straight to the room in which Henry Chartres lay ; but when he was about to enter, a swift descending step on the stair caught his ear, and drew him away just in time to intercept Briscoe, who had finally determined that, wherever he might go, he must leave Snell House that night. Lee peremptorily bade him stay, or he would accuse him of robbery, and send in pursuit; and Briscoe was forced to submit. Lee had been about to ascend the stair again, when Dempster importunately demanded his presence in the dining-room. The latter having made his remarkable communication, Lee intended to arrange with Briscoe some definite plan of action; but another delay took place.

On opening the door of the dining-room, Lee was met by Clacher, whom everybody had forgotten.

'Good evening,' said Clacher, doing it 'Englified,' and walking into the room. His face was streaming with perspiration; his eyes were wild with drink and insanity; his hair hung in wisps about his face.

'Ladies and gentlemen, I am Robert Chartres,' he said. He had remembered what he wanted to do 'Englified.'

'I am bonnie Prince Charlie too,' he added, after a pause. 'I don't understand it. I'm afraid I'm mad but I'm not a fool. I am Robert Chartres.'

Everybody looked at Lee.

He said, 'I don't remember being so intensely interested in my life. How can you possibly hope to succeed in this imposture, Clacher?'

'You're an imposture,' cried Clacher fiercely, staggering a little. 'I'm mad, but I'm no jist a fule, an' naebody daur harm me. Ach!' he hissed, grinding his teeth and shaking his wild hair, enraged at himself for failing to do it 'Englified.' 'I am Robert Chartres,' he shouted, throwing back his head. 'The estate's entailed, and it's mine. I'm bonnie Prince Charlie, too,' he added, more quietly.

'Take a seat,' said Lee. 'Let us all sit down again.'

Clacher stumbled into a chair. Miss Jane forgave Dempster with her eyes, and they sat on a couch together. Muriel stood beside a window with one hand wrapped in the curtain. Briscoe sat opposite Lee, who threw himself back on a large chair on one side of the fireplace. Clacher's chair was against the wall, not far from the door.

'Jane,' said Lee, 'I find no resemblance between this gentleman and Robert. Do you?'

'Not the slightest,' said Miss Jane.

'Do you, Muriel?'

'None.'

'Well, friend,' said Lee, turning to Clacher. 'What have you to say, now?'

'I am Robert Chartres.'

'But none of us recognise you. Recall yourself to our memories in some way.'

'Oh, I'm bonnie Prince Charlie too.'

'That only indicates that you are mad; and a very ordinary madness it is. I am sure there are two or three bonnie Prince Charlies in every lunatic asylum in Scotland.'

'I'm mad, an' naebody daur harm me,' growled Clacher.

'You remember Robert's escapade when he was a boy, Henry?' said Miss Jane.

'To which do you refer? There were so many,' said Lee.

'Oh, not so very many,' said Miss Jane. 'I mean the Inverkip Glen affair.'

'I can't say I do remember it.'

'Oh, you must. You weren't here at the time; but you knew all-about it.'

Lee sat up, and swiftly changed his look of anxiety into a far-reaching glance at the past.

'Ah, yes!' he said, dropping back in his chair again.

'Clacher must have heard about it,' said Miss Jane.

'I shouldn't wonder,' said Lee. 'Clacher, do you know about the Inverkip Glen affair?'

'Of course. I'm Robert Chartres. I'm Clacher too, and Bonnie Prince Charlie. I don't know how.'

'Then,' said Lee, 'just tell us about it. Your acquaintance with it may be evidence of your identity.'

'The Inverkip Glen business?' said Clacher. 'A'body kens that. Damn!' he growled at the Scotch.

'Let us see, now,' said Lee. 'Have you any details that could only be known to Robert and his family?'

'Inverkip Glen,' said Clacher. 'When I was fourteen or thereabouts, I went away wi' a wheen laddies an' hid in it for twa-three days. I ca'ed mysel' Prince Charlie, an' the ithers wis cheeftans—Lochiel an' Glengarry, ye ken. We fought the servants that wis

sent tae bring us hame, an' they had tae send the polis
tae fetch us.'

This was spoken very haltingly, and ended with a
savage oath at his own inability to speak correctly.

' He could have learned all that in the village,' said
Miss Jane.

Lee rose, leant gracefully against the mantelpiece,
and addressed Clacher.

' Clacher,' he said, ' you have unwittingly undertaken a work of art, and for that you deserve high
commendation. You have aspired; you have done your
best. That is sufficient. Success is the only failure.
A compassable aim is an inferior one. Ideals cease to
be when realised. Better succeed in a constant endeavour after the highest, than fail in aspiration to
achieve a result as splendid as any which history
records. These platitudes are not by any means beside
the question, although you don't understand them.'

Here Lee shifted from his easy pose, and stood
firmly on his feet.

' Whatever besides madness,' he continued, ' may
have led you to attempt this imposture, is no concern
of mine. I am only sorry for your sake and my own
that you cannot continue it further. Variety, if not
the soul, is certainly the body of fiction. I hope that,
although you must go out of our story shortly, at least
in your present capacity, you, or some one else in
your sphere of life, may be enmeshed in this web of
circumstance which I help fate to weave. My brother

Robert is at present upstairs. He arrived here this evening.'

Lee looked at all his auditors severally, thoroughly enjoying the effect of this extraordinary news.

'O dear! O dear!' cried Clacher weakly, tedding his hair and fidgeting on his seat. 'Naebody daur harm me, I'm mad.'

'Set your mind at rest, Clacher. Nobody will attempt to harm you.'

'Jane,' he continued, 'it was our unfortunate brother whom we carried upstairs this evening. The woman was his wife.'

Briscoe gasped; but the practical novelist proceeded, smiling, and proud of his ingenuity.

'He has been going by the name of Lee, Maxwell Lee,' he said, staring down Briscoe; 'and makes a scanty living by his pen. His wife is a noble woman, and will not admit his madness; but that he is mad no one else can have any doubt, because the poor fellow imagines that he is me. I will tell you his whole history to-morrow, as far as I know it. I hadn't the remotest idea he was in Scotland until he appeared to-night——'

The droning of a bagpipe not far off, a strange sound at that time of night and in the neighbourhood, interrupted him. A very unskilful attempt at a pibroch succeeded, and as the playing grew more distinct it was evident that the performer approached the house. Muriel raised the window-sash, and the tuneless screaming ceased. Hesitating steps on the gravel were then heard. They stopped opposite the window, and a high, cracked male voice quavered out the first verse of Glen's pathetic ballad, 'Wae's me for Prince Charlie' :—

> ' A wee bird cam tae oor ha' door,
> He warbl't sweet an' clearly ;
> An' aye the o'ercome o' his sang
> Was " Wae's me for Prince Charlie."
> O ! when I heard the bonnie, bonnie bird,
> The tears came drappin' rarely ;
> I took my bonnet off my head,
> For well I lo'ed Prince Charlie ! '

The voice broke entirely at the last line. Said Lee' 'We'll bring this minstrel in,' and left the room. In a few seconds he returned accompanied by a strange figure. It was that of an old man dressed in a ragged Highland costume. His kilt was of the Stuart tartan. His black jacket had been garnished with brass buttons; but of them only a few hung here and there, withered and mouldy; and numerous little tufts of thread on pocket-lids and cuffs and breast showed whence their companions had been shed. His sporran was half-denuded of hair. His hose were holed, and the uppers were parting company with the soles of his shoes. A black feather adorned in a very broken-backed manner his Glengarry bonnet. His pipes he had left in the hall.

There was nothing remarkable in the dress. Such are to be seen any day in the Trongate of Glasgow, the Canongate of Edinburgh, at fairs, or wherever the wandering piper may turn a penny. It was the bear-'

ing of the wearer and the cast of his countenance which commanded attention. As he entered the room he threw back his head, inclining it a little to the left side; his dim grey eyes lightened fitfully, and his gait had something of majesty. He advanced slowly, but without hesitation, and took the seat Lee had vacated.

Of all those in the room Clacher's face indicated the greatest interest.

'Friends,' said the newcomer, keeping on his bonnet, and shaking back his long grey hair, which hung almost to his shoulders, 'I can trust you. "Nowhere beats the heart so kindly as beneath the tartan plaid." You haven't the tartans on, and that is right, for they might betray you. There's a law against the tartan. I wear it in defiance of the law.'

'Wha are ye, man?' cried Clacher, his face undergoing a sudden illumination.

'Do you not know me?' said the stranger. 'You will be true. It is a great sum. Ten thousand pounds. All my own friends have forgotten me. It is strange, strange. I am changed, I know. I am Bonnie Prince Charlie.'

'Ha, ha!' screamed Clacher, 'ha, ha, ha!'

'Two of them,' whispered Dempster to himself, rigid with amazement.

'You astonish me,' said Lee with perfect composure.

'It is sad, I know. I sleep in the woods, and visit

the towns at night. My home is in the bracken. I remember I lived here in 'forty-five. I thought I would revisit the old place to-night. Is not this Scone Palace?'

'No; this is Snell House.'

'Ah! I lived there too, once. But can you tell me this. Why do they accuse me of unfaithfulness? " Flora, when thou wert beside me!" Oh, her eyes were warm and mild like the summer, and her voice made me weep. It is shameful what they say about me. I never loved another.'

Clacher, looking absolutely hideous in his excitement, rushed from his chair, oversetting a small table, and planting himself firmly before the wondering piper, shouted, 'You are Bonnie Prince Charlie?'

'I am. Do me no harm.'

'Then you are Robert Chartres, and you did not commit suicide.'

'I am hungry,' said the Prince.

Clacher pulled from his breast-pocket the crumpled letter he had studied so devoutly in the library, and handing it to Miss Jane, cried: 'It's a' up noo'. I took that letter frae Maister Willum Chartres's pooch whan I fand his corp'. Read it, an' ye'll ken my plot. Gosh, it was a mad yin! Oh, I'm no jist a fule! Naebody daur harm me. An' you, ye scoon'erel,' he screamed, springing behind Lee, and pinning his arms to his body with a hug like a bear's, 'ye're mad, ye're mad. I've turn't the tables on ye, I'm thinking.'

Lee struggled strongly; but Briscoe came to Clacher's help.

'Peter!' exclaimed Lee.

'It's all up, as Clacher says. Every man for himself,' muttered Briscoe. But he wouldn't look Lee in the face.

'You've spoiled a great scene, Peter,' was all Lee said.

'And who is the man upstairs?' asked Muriel, advancing from the window.

'You'll get the key of the bedroom in which he is in this pocket,' said Briscoe, indicating by an uncouth gesture a pocket in his coat, as he did not wish to release his hold on Lee.

Muriel took the key and left the room.

Miss Jane read and re-read the letter given her by Clacher, and was still considering it when Muriel returned with her father. He was not long awake, and had to be supported by his daughter. Miss Jane recognised him at once and kissed his cheek. There was no exclaiming. When they came out of it they would know from their exhaustion how excited they had been. The tears stood in Muriel's eyes, and her face was very pale, but serenity marked every lineament.

'Where is Mrs. Lee?' asked Henry Chartres when he had got seated.

At that moment Caroline entered the room. She had remained in the bedroom Lee had appropriated,

afraid lest her interference might precipitate some rash
act on the part of her husband or her brother; but the
bagpipes, the singing, the opening and shutting of
doors, and the loud voices downstairs intimated a crisis
of some kind, and she had concluded at last to have a
share in it, hoping to prevent disaster to her husband,
as she judged from the noise that his control of circumstances had come to an end.   As Caroline entered,
the two gardeners and the coachman appeared at the
door, Muriel having sent for them at her father's
request.

Muriel looked at Mrs. Lee for a second or two as if
debating some question with herself, and then noise-
lessly left the room.   She couldn't keep Frank waiting
any longer.

'Maxwell Lee,' said Henry Chartres, 'for your
wife's sake you go scot free.   She has told me all about
you.   As for you, Peter Briscoe, your present action
shows what you are.   Take him and duck him well in
the horse-pond.'

The coachman and the gardeners, nothing loath,
approached Briscoe; but Lee, having regained his
liberty, put himself before his brother-in-law in an
attitude of defence.

'I beg you, sir, not to insist on this,' he said in a
passion of intercession; 'it is mere revenge.   I entreat
you.'

'But he betrayed you,' said Chartres.

'Well, I suppose the world puts it that way.   But

he merely acted independently and without due consideration. That has been the fault of this work all along : the principal collaborateurs have been too frequently out of harmony. Since he has chosen to bring our story to a sudden end in this way, I have no right to complain. Do not damage your character for magnanimity which these events have developed so remarkably—a result very gratifying to me—by a petty revenge on my brother-in-law.'

Chartres signed to the servants to retire. ' You are a strange man,' he said.

' Miss Chartres,' said Lee, ' in token that you cherish no deep-rooted feeling against me, will you oblige me by reading that letter ? '

Miss Jane looked at her brother ; he assented, and she read :—

' My dear William,—You will be astonished, not very agreeably, I am afraid, to learn that I am still in the land of the living. I have been in a state of abject poverty for years. I will not trouble you with the particulars of my wretched career. I have burnt up my stomach with drink. Insanity has addled my brain. I am a beggar, and go about the country—I am ashamed to say it for your sake—playing the bagpipes. In my mad fits I have repeatedly tried to commit suicide. At present I am quite sane; the only difficulty I have is to reconcile my being Robert Chartres with the fact that I am also Bonnie Prince Charlie. I write this in London; and I am going to start at once and at last to try and come to you. It would be better to kill myself; but I am too great a coward when I am sane. I want to enjoy comfort once more before I die. If I do not reach you within a month after this letter, I think you may conclude that I am dead.

> 'I am, your brother,
>> 'ROBERT CHARTRES.'

All eyes turned on the writer of the letter. He was fast asleep in his chair, smiling like a child.

'Briscoe,' said Lee, you recognised and submitted to the *deus ex machinâ* at once. I would have fought longer, and might yet have conquered. I am sorry the conclusion is so inartistic, so improbable. There is nothing more absurd than reality. Clacher, my fine fellow, you played a bold game; as the attempt of a mad rascal it was very fair. What a lot of mad people there are! How small the world is! Ah!' he cried, as Frank and Muriel entered, 'my good lovers! I believe you are even now thanking me for my opposition.'

'Who is this young gentleman?' asked Mr. Chartres.

'Oh! I found him at the north wall; I knew he would be there,' said Muriel, radiant, and scarcely knowing what she said.

'Do you frequently find young gentlemen and bring them here in this way?'

' Oh, papa! His name is Frank Hay, and we are going to be married.'

' I have never seen your like, Muriel,' said Lee, leaving the room. Briscoe followed him, bestowing a surly nod on Dempster. But Caroline before she went timidly kissed the hand of the injured man.

THE END

PRINTED BY
SPOTTISWOODE AND CO., NEW-STREET SQUARE
LONDON

Manchester Guardian.

'It is quite certain that anyone who reads the first chapter will read on to the end of the book without skipping a line.'

The Speaker.

'Sincerely and engagingly human; and while it makes you laugh—even at the very moment when it makes you laugh—it comes perilously near to making you weep also.'

The World.

'Cleverly written Mr. John Davidson's book certainly is, and the scenes between the Provost of Mintern and Cosmo Mortimer are extremely comical.'

The Academy.

'Mr. Davidson has indisputably the gift of style.'

Athenæum.

'For those who can enjoy the absolutely grotesque— a prose extravaganza somewhat in the Gilbertian style— the career of Ninian Jameson will provide a good deal of amusement.'